RETURN TO LOVE

Sally Marsden is a girl who once had everything she wanted: a promising career as a model and Mike, a photographer, for a boyfriend — until the car accident which subjects her to months of hospital treatment for facial injuries. With her career cut short, a skiing holiday in the Austrian Alps provides a change of perspective. From here on, a young ski instructor, Johann, starts to play a major role in Sally's recovery; but by an unfortunate coincidence, Mike arrives at the same resort . . .

PATRICIA ROBINS

RETURN TO LOVE

Complete and Unabridged

LINFORD
Leicester

First published in Great Britain in 1968

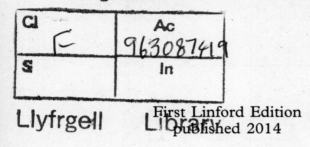

First Linford Edition
published 2014

A catalogue record for this book is available
from the British Library.

ISBN 978–1–4448–2156–7

Published by
F. A. Thorpe (Publishing)
Anstey, Leicestershire

Set by Words & Graphics Ltd.
Anstey, Leicestershire
Printed and bound in Great Britain by
T. J. International Ltd., Padstow, Cornwall

This book is printed on acid-free paper

1

She sat with the left side of her face to the carriage window. She had done so automatically. The concealment of the deep red scar was part of her normal pattern of behaviour now. The habit had not taken so long to form. Now, two years after the accident, her choice of position whenever she was in the presence of other people unconsciously placed the unscarred side of her face to them.

The boat train taking Sally Marsden and her friend, Bobbie Crowther, to Dover from Victoria, passed through a tunnel as it neared the coast. For a moment the window glass, darkened outside, assumed a mirror-like quality and Sally's slim body stiffened. One hand reached quickly to her cheek, covering the disfigurement of which she was now instantly aware.

The happy, carefree mood which had engulfed her since their departure an hour earlier, left her to be replaced by the old familiar despair. The ski-ing holiday in Austria, to which she had so looked forward for months, once again assumed the proportions of a nightmare. There would be so many people to face; to stare at her; to ask questions perhaps; to offer sympathy; pity. How much easier to have stayed at home, in the flat where Bobbie alone could see her. Bobbie was far too familiar with her disfigurement even to notice it any more. She, Sally, could relax with Bobbie; and at work where she had her own tiny box-like little office next door to dear, kind old Mr Saunders, the lawyer. He never stared! And Cocky, the lad who brought in the mail and the tea, was far too self-conscious about the terrible state of acne from which he suffered to be bothered about her.

Sally glanced at the other passengers in the carriage. There were two business men with briefcases, one lost in his newspaper, the other checking some lists. Neither was concerned with her. Nor was the middle-aged woman on her right who had fallen asleep shortly after leaving London. Opposite her, Bobbie was deep in a paperback, her round freckled face absorbed, the reddish hair falling over one eye, obscuring half her face.

Sally's hand went to her own hair. Long, fair, smooth and silky, it hung like a curtain across the damaged cheek. As it was, she could hide behind that curtain of hair and unless a wind blew it away from her face or she forgot and swept it back thoughtlessly behind one ear, no one noticed the scar.

'You've got such a THING about it!' Bobbie had reproved her so often that the words were all but meaningless now. 'You shouldn't be so conscious of it. No one notices it. They only stare because you're so pretty.'

Sally drew a long sigh. It was true that she had been pretty — *once*. Three years ago, she had been able to accept

3

that people stared at her because they found something attractive in her large green eyes or in the tilt of her nose or the shape of her face. She was not conceited but even at school it had been impossible to avoid this knowledge when all her friends told her she ought to be a model with her looks and figure. Then, meeting Mike, being swept off her feet by him, being turned into a top model almost overnight — she had accepted the simple fact of her beauty gratefully. Since the accident she had read through the scrap-book of cuttings Aunt Margaret had kept religiously throughout the fantastic year of her success. *'A seventeen-year-old with the poise of a woman ten years older!'* *'Young, fresh, beautiful, dreamy, mysterious!'* *'Eyes like an Egyptian Princess and a figure that puts Madonna to shame!'* There were so many! Exaggerated, no doubt, but flattering. Not that the printed words meant anything to her in those days — not when she had Mike's voice at her ear telling her how beautiful she seemed to him. That was all that mattered — that he admired her; that he loved her; needed her; wanted her.

Sally's hands clenched in her lap as she sat now oblivious to the train, the carriage, to Bobbie, remembering the accident that had changed her life so completely. It was the night Mike had said he was in love with her, wanted to share his life with her, would marry her. He'd made a great deal of money because of her — his work with Sally was in ever-increasing demand and his own career as a fashion photographer was at last established. She believed he had 'created' her, but Mike always said it was the other way round. 'We're on our way to the top,' he had said confidently. 'You and me, babe. We've done it!' Mike had a new white Porsche parked outside his flat and he wanted to go out and celebrate. Somewhere in the suburbs of London, Mike had taken a corner too sharply. The car skidded on the wet road and they had hit a parked car head-on . . .

Sally shivered. She did not want to remember yet again those first terrible weeks in hospital; the finding out how badly her face had been cut; the slow painful discovery that it might be months, even years, before plastic surgery could right the damage. Perhaps hardest of all to bear was Mike's terrible remorse. His visits to the hospital — at first so desperately, eagerly awaited, became each time a little more painful. He refused to accept that the accident was not altogether his fault; that if it had not been raining so heavily the car might not have skidded, that the owner of the other car should not have parked it so near the turning. The case was heard in court and Mike judged guilty. He was driving too fast and he had been drinking — not much but enough to hold against him. It reinforced his belief in his own guilt and he tortured himself and Sally with self-recriminations.

Aunt Margaret insisted upon engaging a lawyer — old Mr Saunders — for Sally. Aunt Margaret said she must, whether she wished it or not (and she was still a minor), claim against Mike for damages she had received in the accident. Nothing Sally said to her aunt, who was also her guardian, could dissuade her from taking a case against Mike. His insurance company, not he, would pay, she said over and over again. Sally must realise that her career as a model would cease — at any rate for a year or two. She would be many months in hospital on and off, having plastic surgery. She would need money.

Mike agreed. He wanted to give her everything he owned. Anything to make up for the ugly scar that ran down her cheek, slightly puckering one corner of her mouth.

For several weeks he did no work. Sally at last persuaded him to use another model to take over her own commitments. Mike gave Sally's work to Jess — a young half Indian girl he had known before he met Sally. Gradually Mike's visits became scarcer. Sally knew he was frantically busy catching up on lost time and tried not to be hurt. When he did come, he was as loving as ever but always with that tormented look of guilt on his face. She hoped each time before he came into the room that this next time he saw her, his eyes would not go to her face. If he could only forget — just for a few minutes — what he had done to her! Then she, too, might be able to forget it; to relegate it to the role of unimportance. But it was important to him and, through him, to her. She began to find little ways to hide her face from him, altering her hair style; keeping the visitor's chair on the other side of the bed; hunching her knees and cupping both cheeks with her hands.

It was Aunt Margaret who brought things to a head.

'You're always in floods of tears after his visits, Sally! I can't bear to see you so unhappy. What's wrong?'

That was when she realised for the first time that she must let Mike go. He was bound to her now not from love but from guilt. He was ashamed of what he had done to her and made her ashamed of herself. As to the girl, Jess — Mike had once said: 'It's because we are in love we work so perfectly together, Sally. You anticipate my needs and I am in tune with your moods. It's like a painter with his model — the closer they are in spirit, in body, in thought, the more perfectly can he reproduce her. A photographer feels the same way.'

Now he was working in close harmony with Jess. How long before he needed to be close to *her?* Perhaps already he had held her in his arms, kissed her? Made love to her?

Knowing she would never be able to model again she told him she had accepted the fact that they no longer had a future together. He had sworn he still loved her; that he would never love anyone else, yet in the end, he had stopped visiting her. In a way, she had been happier then for his visits were too much of a strain and she loved him far, far too much to be able to bear each tiny step away from her.

There had followed a period of convalescence with Aunt Margaret in her little cottage in Sussex. Then the first of the plastic surgery operations in East Grinstead hospital. Sally had welcomed the pain and discomfort — it helped her to forget the worse pain of a life without Mike. Aunt Margaret had got her a job with Mr Saunders — the perfect job since apart from her modelling, which Mike had taught her, she had nothing but her secretarial qualifications. And Mr Saunders' dingy little offices in the Temple offered a refuge, a hiding place, from the stares of the world. In a firm or factory or other big concern, she would have been forced to face people.

Three months ago the case against Mike had been heard. The judge,

kindly and sympathetic, had neverthe-
less insisted upon seeing Sally's scar.
The day had been an ordeal — one she
would have forfeited willingly, but Aunt
Margaret had been satisfied with the
outcome. Sally had been awarded full
compensation and the judge had
suggested that as soon as possible,
Sally should go on holiday and try to
forget the whole unfortunate affair.
Aunt Margaret had advised her to
invest the large sum of money
awarded, but agreed with the judge
that Sally should keep back enough to
pay for a really good holiday.

Because of her former fame as a
model, the press had been present and
Sally had had to contend with publicity
she had once craved but now abhorred.
For days afterwards, she woke at night
in a cold sweat, trying in her nightmare
to avoid the flash of photographers'
bulbs.

She now lived in a tiny two-roomed
flat with Bobbie — an old school
friend. It was Bobbie who thought up

the idea of a ski-ing holiday. She brought home the pamphlets and booklets and swamped Sally with literature and admonitions that she should do what the judge said — have a really good holiday.

'You're far too thin and pale and nervy, Sal. You *need* a holiday — a complete change. You need to get out and about and have a good time. Do you realise you haven't seen anyone but me, Aunt Margaret and that stuffy old boss of yours in *months!* I'd give my right arm to have the chance of a holiday and here you are shaking your head and saying 'no'. I wish I had the chance!'

So Sally had conceived the idea of going with Bobbie — for her friend's sake rather than her own. Bobbie had been so patient, so understanding; always trying to include her on double dates yet never forcing her against her will; going with her to the theatre or cinema or for Sunday walks in Kew Gardens or just staying home in the flat to keep her company. Bobbie was the perfect, unselfish, undemanding friend.

'I must try to enjoy myself — for Bobbie's sake!' Sally told herself as the train came to an abrupt halt just outside Dover.

It began to reverse and travel downwards towards the harbour. Bobbie put down her book and glanced eagerly out of the window.

'We're nearly there!' she cried. 'Isn't it *exciting*, Sal? I've never been abroad before, I can hardly believe it's really and truly about to happen!'

Sally smiled but as she did so, she pulled the soft curtain of fair hair a little further forward over her cheek, and adopting a fashionable style, tied the pink silk scarf over her head and round her throat.

⋆ ⋆ ⋆

They found their way, with the rest of the passengers from the train, through customs on to the cross-Channel ferry.

13

The boat was only half full and they found seats on B Deck in the lounge without any trouble. They both wanted to buy duty-free perfume so, as soon as it was permitted, they made their way, following the signs, to the ship's shop. As Sally was paying for hers, using her English currency to do so, a young man on her right-hand side spoke to her.

'Do you know if I can get my duty-free spirits here?' he asked.

Without thinking, Sally swung round to reply to him but his gaze had turned to the row of bottles behind her and without looking at her again he hurried away before Sally could speak.

The hot colour flooded her cheeks. In her mind there was no doubt that the man had been thoroughly disconcerted by the sight of the scar on her face. In the pre-accident days, she had become accustomed to boys and men trying to strike up an acquaintance with her. It had always amused Mike — and made him just a little jealous — to see how instantly she attracted the opposite sex. Now it was all different . . . and the incident, unimportant enough in itself, flung her back into a depression that even Bobbie's determined good spirits could not revive. She wished desperately that she had stayed at home. Nothing could have been more stupid than to lay herself open to situations such as this. It was pointless for Bobbie to say: 'I think he was trying to pick you up, Sal!' The man himself and his motives were irrelevant. The only salient fact was that he had run away — as most people must want to run away when they saw her scarred face.

Sally joined Bobbie in the self-service café for tea. They had been warned by the travel agency that there was no restaurant on the night train that would carry them to Austria and they intended buying sandwiches and cheese and biscuits for their supper to eat later on the train. When they had discussed it in the privacy of the flat, the idea of picnicking in a sleeper had seemed such fun. Now Sally could raise no enthusiasm. For Bobbie's sake she tried to seem cheerful, and at the same time, keep the scarf more firmly round her face. The one careless moment at the shop had put her on her guard. She would not let it slip again until she and Bobbie were safely alone in the sleeper.

It was nearly seven in the evening before they were exploring the third-class compartment on the all-night train to Zürs. Because it was only half full, they had the carriage to themselves and the friendly French attendant told them he would not make up their bunks until later so that they would have more room for the meal.

Sally took off her jacket and removed her shoes, tucking her long beautiful legs beneath her as she curled herself into a corner. She was beginning to relax now she was alone with Bobbie. But her thoughts would not stop wandering. She was remembering Mike — remembering how he had promised a honeymoon on the Continent.

'I've never made love on a train!' he'd told her, his blue eyes twinkling with amusement. 'I think we'll have to try it, Sal. We'll have a first-class compartment and bribe the attendant not to disturb us till morning.'

But it wasn't Mike here with her now — just Bobbie, cheerful, friendly, happy Bobbie. And Mike would never make love to her — not on a train, not anywhere . . .

In six months' time Sally was to have the last, so they hoped, plastic surgery operation. By the time it was over and healed, there would be only the barest trace of the scar — and what faint traces might remain would be easily covered by make-up. It would be as if the accident had never happened . . . except this time there would be no Mike. That scar could never be healed. She and Mike had been so close . . . so instantly in accord with one another. It was the perfect relationship, combining their careers, their hopes, their feelings, their desires.

17

'Oh, Sal, *look!*' Bobbie cried, pushing her magazine into her friend's hands. 'Surely that's your ex-boyfriend. There on the left! Michael Chancery. That's him, isn't it? And that must be the girl who models for him now. Isn't she stunning!'

'Yes, beautiful!' Sally's calm voice hid the turmoil of her thumping heart, her trembling hands. It *was* Mike, smiling into the camera, his own favourite Leica held loosely against his chest, his brown hair curling into his neck and falling over his forehead. He looked smarter than when she had last seen him — more relaxed. His Armani suit fitted perfectly. In the caption below, she read: *Jess, Chancery's new and favourite model, wearing a Jasper Conran suit; hair style by Liam at Molton Brown.*

Yes, the girl was beautiful with dark, slanting oriental eyes and a long slender body that was flowing and supple, and somehow essentially feminine.

'She's more attractive than I ever was!'

18

Sally thought. And then, as always, when she found herself remembering Jess and Mike together, she shut her mind firmly against such imaginings. The pain of supposing what might be between them was too much for her to bear. To be without Mike was bad enough. To think of him in love with Jess . . .

'Let's eat!' she said brightly to Bobbie. 'I'm starving!'

But whilst her friend eagerly unpacked the supper they had chosen with such care in the cafeteria, Sally knew that she could not eat more than a token amount of food. The effort it had cost her to come out of her retirement into the public eye was taking its toll on her nervous system. She felt exhausted — and unable to give way to that fatigue which she realised her friend could not possibly understand. Bobbie knew that Sally shunned company and accepted her anti-social behaviour as inevitable, but she had no real idea how much strength of will it required for Sally even to do the shopping on a Saturday morning.

Bobbie bit into a chicken sandwich and looked at her friend with sparkling eyes.

'This is great, isn't it? And I owe it all to you. You'll never know how grateful I am. I know you didn't *think* you wanted to come but now you're here, you have to admit it's terrific. We're actually in France! Isn't it wonderful? And when we wake up tomorrow, we'll be in Austria — just think! I know I ought not to be so happy — not when I remember *why* you've got all that money. Still, it's nearly over, isn't it! By Christmas no one will know you ever had an accident, and as to Mike — well, you're better off without him, aren't you? If he'd *really* loved you, he'd never have let you break up . . . '

'Yes!' thought Sally. Bobbie, with unintentional brutality had spoken the truth. And the truth was the hardest part of all to bear.

2

Between waking next morning and their arrival at Lengen where they would disembark, Bobbie struck up an acquaintance with an Australian couple who had the adjoining sleeping compartment. They, too, were on their way to Zürs and Bobbie was hopping with excitement.

'They're going to the same hotel — the Edelweiss!' she told Sally as she begged her to come out into the corridor and meet her new friends. 'They're really nice, Sal, and they seem to know just where to catch the bus from Lengen to Zürs. *Do* come and meet them.'

Sally dabbed a little more powder over her cheek and tied the pink scarf round her face. It did not hide the scar completely, for that stretched from her left temple to her lower jaw, but it concealed most of it.

As Bobbie had said, the Australian couple were friendly, middle-aged, with children Sally's and Bobbie's age they had left behind in Sydney where they lived. If they noticed Sally's face, they did not stare or make any comment. Sally relaxed and her spirits rose. It was a beautiful morning, the sun pouring in through the train windows and she had had a surprisingly good night's sleep. Not even the thought of Mike and Jess had kept her awake.

Their new friends, Melville and Jean Tompson, had a thermos of coffee in their compartment which they shared with the girls. The journey passed quickly and by ten-thirty, they were climbing out on to the platform at Lengen. The bus was waiting — a rack on the back full of skis; people in ski-clothes already aboard. The air was very cold but the sun shone down on them from a totally cloudless blue sky.

The Australians helped the two girls sort out their Austrian money so they could purchase their bus tickets. They sat down in pairs of seats behind each other. The bus started its upward climb, its wheels heavily chained, the snow piled six feet high on either side of the road.

It was some minutes before Sally turned her gaze from the view of the snow-covered valley up which they were travelling and became aware of the young man staring across the aisle at her. He was very tall — over six foot, with straight fair hair and blue-grey eyes in a very sun-tanned face. He was wearing dark navy salopettes and a navy and white crew-necked sweater beneath a red and white anorak. As Sally met his eyes, he smiled. Embarrassed, she looked quickly away but not before Bobbie had kicked her leg unobtrusively and muttered:

'Isn't he gorgeous! I bet he's not English!'

No, Sally thought, he did not look in the least English. She had to agree in her mind that Bobbie was right — he was very good-looking, but what Bobbie did not seem to understand was that she didn't want a boyfriend. She had finished with love. It was too painful a memory for her ever to wish to revive the experience. Besides, the young man sitting so near her could only see the right side of her face. When he saw her scar . . . she could already feel the awkwardness of that moment when, since like most people probably he was kind, he would try not to turn away too quickly.

For half an hour the bus, in low gear, took them upwards along the valley, past one tiny village, through two dark tunnels carved in the rocky mountain-side, and at last into the tiny village of Zürs. It was exactly like a picture post-card village, nestling between mountain ranges on either side. Austrian-type chalets and hotels bordered the road. Everywhere there were skiers — in the snow-covered streets, on the slopes, sitting outside the hotels on benches in the sun; standing at the strange little three-sided outdoor bar, drinking, talking, laughing.

'I'll learn to ski really well!' Sally thought as she watched the bird-like figures weaving gracefully down towards them. 'I'll concentrate on it — get really good. It'll give me something to do — something to work at.'

The next moment the two girls were climbing down from the bus and the hotel porter was loading their luggage and that of the Australians on to a sledge.

Sally followed Bobbie and the Australians across the road towards the hotel entrance. Suddenly the rubber soles of the fur boots she was wearing slipped on the icy surface. She stumbled and would have fallen but for an arm grasping her round the waist and holding her upright.

'Fräulein?'

She looked up to see the young man from the bus staring down at her anxiously.

'Thank you. How silly of me. I nearly fell!' she said stupidly in English. The grey-blue eyes smiled.

'It is more easy to stand in the ski-boots!' he said in a strongly accented English. 'You permit that I hold your arm so — to the hotel?'

It was impossible to refuse such a quaint and polite request. The colour high in her cheeks, Sally allowed him to lead her forward. At the door of the hotel through which Bobbie and the Australians had already disappeared, her companion released her arm, bowed and said:

'*Aufweidersehen!*' Before she could thank him he was gone.

Sally walked towards the reception desk, her mind and thoughts confused. How exciting life would be if there'd been no accident, no scar. Maybe with a charming young man like the one she had just met, she could have had a wonderful time here in Zürs. Bobbie always made friends wherever she went; she was fun, amusing, friendly and the boys all liked her. They, the two of them, could have joined up with parties of people their own age and . . . but

26

what was the use of dreaming? If there'd been no accident, no scar, she'd have been married to Mike by now, sharing his penthouse flat in the Strand, working hard, looking after him, loving him. There'd be no need for an attractive young man to take her mind and thoughts off Mike.

'Room 76 on the fourth floor,' Bobbie broke in on her thoughts. 'I've got the key. Shall we go up?'

Their room was simply but comfortably furnished. Outside the French windows, a balcony held sun chairs and the view over the mountains to either side was breathtaking. Bobbie was dancing about with excitement.

'Isn't it great, Sal? And come and see this funny bath — it's only half a bath, really. You have to sit in it!'

It was a kind of hip bath in which it was impossible to lie full length but neither girl minded — it was a luxury having their own private bathroom.

Their luggage was brought up and both girls changed into the new ski suits they had bought at home. Bobbie wore violet salopettes and matching anorak over a pink sweater. Sally's outfit was black with a heavy white sweater with a black, white and ochre patterned yoke. She brushed out her fair hair and began to wind a black chiffon scarf turban-wise round her face and beneath her chin.

Bobbie eyed her friend speculatively.

'Are you really going to wear that thing?' she asked. 'It looks great on you but — oh, Sal, if only you'd forget about that silly old scar!'

Sally's mouth tightened.

'I can't forget it, Bobbie. Let me work things out my own way. Does it really look all right? I'll wear something else if it looks silly!'

Bobbie sighed.

'No, it doesn't look silly. You're so attractive you can wear anything and it just looks glamorous. It's just that . . . well, I know it isn't any of my business but isn't it sort of asking for trouble to pretend? That there's nothing wrong, I mean?' She stammered in her effort to put what she wanted to say tactfully. 'I mean, if you didn't try to hide the scar, then you'd know right at the start who minded about it and who didn't — that guy in the bus, for instance. Because you covered your face up, he doesn't know what you really look like.'

Sally stared at her reflection in the glass, her eyes bitter.

'You mean, he wouldn't have been so friendly if he'd seen me as I really am?'

'No, I didn't mean that!' Bobbie said crossly, stamping her foot on the bare polished boards. 'You don't seem to realise that you're pretty enough even with the scar to attract people. But now, if you meet him again it'll be a shock because you did hide it. It would sort of make him think it is worse than if he'd seen it right away.'

'Well, I really don't care what that guy — or anyone thinks!' Sally said, straightening her shoulders and turning away from the mirror. 'I've come here to ski, Bobbie, and that's what I intend to do. Let's go and hire our skis and boots now — then we can start ski-ing after lunch. I can't wait, can you?'

Bobbie, easily diverted, fell in with Sally's suggestion. They went downstairs and were directed to a funny little shop adjoining the hotel where skis were hired, mended, waxed, repaired and stored. Sally, who had been studying German in preparation for the holiday, managed to make it understood that she and Bobbie required equipment. They were both a bit shaken at the bill presented to them when at last they were equipped with appropriately sized skis and boots.

'Never mind!' Sally said as they left the shop to go back into the hotel for lunch. 'This is one holiday when we needn't worry about costs. We aren't paying from our own savings, are we?'

The hotel seemed full. As the girls went into the dining-room, their new Australian friends waved to them and invited them to share their window table. Sally, conscious of the stares that followed her and Bobbie across the room, sat down gratefully with her back to the rest of the diners.

'Do forgive me for being personal,' said Jean, 'but you move so beautifully. Are you a dancer by any chance?'

Before Sally could reply, Bobbie broke in, explaining that Sally had been a model until her accident. To Sally's surprise, neither Jean nor Melville Tompson seemed particularly concerned when Bobbie mentioned the scar which now made modelling impossible — or at least until the plastic surgery was completed.

'Oh, we noticed it on the train. Poor you!' Jean said without a trace of pity in her voice. 'It'll probably be a lot less obvious when you get tanned by the mountain sun. If it keeps as hot as this, you'll need to cover your face with oil before you go out on the slopes. And you must have sun goggles, too — the glare is awful and bad for your eyes.'

Melville Tompson, a large, heavily

built man with a lined jolly face, told the girls in his fatherly fashion, that they must join a ski school.

'Everyone does out here!' he said. 'The Austrians take their ski-ing very seriously and the standard of teaching is excellent. You'll be in the beginners' class, of course, but if you pick it up quickly, you might get promoted.'

'Can't you ski alone?' Sally asked.

Both husband and wife looked at her in surprise.

'Well, you can — yes! But it's more fun in a class — you meet people — make friends. And it's not too strenuous — from ten till lunch-time and then from two to four o'clock.'

After lunch Bobbie tried to talk Sally into following their new friends' advice. But Sally refused to be persuaded.

'You join the class, Bobbie. I'd rather ski by myself, I don't want to get embroiled with a lot of other people.'

'Well, if you won't, I won't!' Bobbie said flatly, but Sally argued:

'We're together a great deal at home, Bobbie — it would probably be a good thing for us not to be together *all* the time out here. Besides, I'll only be a drag — you know I can't help wanting to avoid people. Let me enjoy myself in my own way, Bobbie, please. I'll be perfectly happy on my own. I *like* being alone. *Please.*'

Reluctantly Bobbie agreed they should go their separate ways — at least for this afternoon and the next day — 'until we see how things work out,' she said. She left Sally and accompanied the Australians across the road to where the classes for the ski school were gathering in their different groups. Sally went up to her room and stood on the balcony watching. She made out what she took to be the ski instructors in blue ski-pants and red anoraks with white markings. It was too far away for her to be certain but she thought she could make out Bobbie bending down as she adjusted the fastening of her heavy ski-boots.

The sun was still burning down fiercely but it was moving westward and it would not be very long before it dropped behind the high snow-covered mountain on her right.

'Perhaps I won't ski today!' Sally thought. 'I'll sit here in the sun on my balcony; maybe write home to Aunt Margaret.'

The groups of skiers were moving away now in different directions. Soon the meeting area was deserted and Sally had the feeling of being kept in at school — of not being allowed to join the other girls at play. She told herself not to be so stupid. It was her own fault she was by herself. She'd *wanted* to be alone. Yet now she had succeeded, she was strangely lonely.

She unwound the scarf and covered her face with sun oil. Then she sat down on the balcony in a deck-chair and closed her eyes. She could feel the heat burning into her and wondered if Jean was right — that the scar would be less obvious in a suntanned face. Her natural skin colouring was so fair, the livid red was obvious, ugly. Maybe if she could turn a golden brown . . .

The sudden drop in temperature as the sun moved westward leaving the balcony in shade woke Sally from a deep sleep. Her face felt tight and hot but the air was cold enough to make her shiver. Hurriedly she went into the room, closing the French windows behind her. Bobbie's bedside clock pointed to three-thirty. Another half-hour before Bobbie returned.

Sally put back the scarf after wiping the oil from her face and putting on fresh make-up. She washed her hands and went downstairs to the lounge where she busied herself writing post-cards. On an impulse she sent one to Mike — the first time she had communicated with him since their break up. But it was not with any idea of renewing their meetings — it was just to let him know in a casual way that she was having a wonderful time

— without him.

She slipped the card into the hotel post-box before she could change her mind.

People were beginning to come back into the hotel now. Their faces were glowing as they ordered beers or tea served in glasses with lemon or hot chocolate with great blobs of whipped cream on top.

Sally heard several English voices but there seemed to be every nationality in the hotel — Austrians, Germans, French, American, Danish. She felt cut-off — the odd man out, and was glad when Bobbie appeared with the Australians.

They all ordered hot chocolate and then Bobbie regaled them with her first attempts at ski-ing — how she'd sat down far more often than she had stood up; how a funny little German man had told her she had no right to 'smell' at him.

'Of course he meant 'smile',' Bobbie explained, giggling, 'but he pronounced it wrong and it only made me laugh the more until I fell over again. Oh, Sally, we've the most fabulous instructor — absolutely marvellous with a great sense of humour. His English is so funny. And there's a smashing English boy called Basil, of all names! He's been here three days already and he says our hotel has a marvellous tea-dance at five o'clock. He wants us to go to it — it's downstairs where that sign says 'Bar — Dancing'. You will come, won't you, Sal?'

She was on the point of refusing when Melville broke in, saying:

'Of course, we'll all come down. Sounds fun. Though I reckon I'm going to be pretty stiff tomorrow if I don't have a hot bath right away.'

Sally did not feel able to excuse herself from the dance without seeming churlish. She knew Bobbie would be unhappy if she didn't go, although it was the last thing she herself wanted. If Bobbie's new boyfriend came and asked her to dance and Melville danced with his wife, she'd be sitting alone at the table and . . .

'I can't dance!' Jean was saying in her broad Australian accent. 'Never learned and never wanted to. But Melville loves to dance. He's good, too. You'll partner him, won't you Sally?'

They found a table a little way from the four-piece band which seemed to think it had to play at maximum volume. The large underground room was crowded and the noise and heat phenomenal. But it was fun, too. As Jean had promised, Melville was an excellent dancer and Sally, who had once thought of taking up dancing as a profession, really began to enjoy herself.

'You're good!' Melville said as he led her back to the table to rejoin his wife. Bobbie was still on the floor with a long, lanky boy she'd introduced as her Basil! 'You're as light as a feather. Sal's quite a dancer, Jean,' he informed his wife.

'I could see. I was watching,' Jean said, smiling.

Suddenly, there was a movement at Sally's elbow.

Someone stood with his back to her, talking to Melville.

'Please to excuse that I ask the permission to dance with your lady?'

Sally's face flushed. She was almost sure she recognised the voice — the long thin body . . .

Melville was looking bewildered.

'My lady?' he echoed. 'I'm afraid my wife doesn't dance — oh, you mean Sally?' The young man turned and bowed to Sally.

'You will permit?' he asked.

The last tune had ended and the band was now playing an old fashioned waltz.

'I . . . I haven't danced this for years!' Sally said. 'I don't know if . . . '

'Is the Viennese waltz. I am from Vienna. I like very much to dance if you permit?'

She could not refuse. She stood up

and a moment later, his arm was round her and she was gliding round the room with her partner. He moved effortlessly, beautifully, every movement completely controlled and yet supple and perfectly in time to the music. Sally, at first anxious and tense, felt herself relax. She closed her eyes and gave herself up completely to the dance. She had not the slightest difficulty in following him, although he held her quite far from him.

When the music finally ended, she opened her eyes to find him smiling down at her.

'I have not in seven years danced so good with my partner. Girls are not good dancers any more. You are a good dancer!'

Sally smiled.

'That's because you lead so well,' she said. 'I *did* enjoy that.'

Unthinkingly she brushed her hand across her face which was hot and sticky, moving the scarf and the concealing hair away from her cheek. It was too late when, a second after, she realised that she had revealed the scar. He was already aware of it.

'You have had the ski-ing accident?' he asked.

She covered her cheek quickly with her hand, unable now to look at him.

'No, I don't ski. It was a car accident . . . ' she stammered. She wasn't used to people mentioning her disfigurement.

'But you must ski. If you are a good dancer, you make also the good skier. It is the same thing — the movement. I not speak so good English but you understand, no?'

His words confused her. He seemed disinterested in her accident. She tried to concentrate on what he was saying.

'Is not possible for me to understand you where is so much noise. You permit I take you to the bar? Is next door. There is quieter and we can have a drink.'

She paused uncertainly, but a glance across to their table showed Melville

41

and Jean deep in conversation and Bobbie still absent.

'All right — thank you!'

But before they reached the door, the band had begun to play a soft dreamy melody, strange to Sally but apparently well known to her companion. He paused, looking down at her smiling.

'I would like very much to dance this. You permit?'

Amused and not a little confused, Sally nodded. It seemed to be an English tune — 'Spanish Eyes' — which the band leader sang. Her companion chose a mixture of a slow foxtrot and rumba step which she did not know but which she was able to follow without difficulty. He did not talk as he danced, but concentrated on what he was doing as if he were only half aware that he even had a partner.

When it was over and they were sitting up at the bar, Sally said:

'You really love dancing, don't you?'

'Yes! And for you also the dancing is

important, no? How is it I should call you? I will introduce myself, but my surname is much difficult for English peoples to pronounce, so please just to call me Johann?'

Sally smiled.

'And I am Sally.'

'This is a name I do not hear before. Much Joans and Patricias and Susans and Lindas, but never do I hear Sally. Is a real name or how do you say — funny name?'

'No, it's really my real name!' Sally said. She had completely forgotten about her face, her nervousness, her now habitual shyness. She was perfectly at ease until he said:

'Is pity that you have this motor-car accident. It spoil so lovely the face. In the bus this morning I tell myself, Johann, this is most beautiful girl ever you did see. You do not smile at me. I think you have the very unhappy eyes. It makes you sad that you are not most beautiful girl on this side of your face any more?'

His words were so direct, so child-ishly simple and without trace of underlying pity or sympathy, she was able to answer him directly.

'Yes, it has made me unhappy. I realise that it is difficult for people to enjoy looking at me now.'

'This I do not think.'

She was suddenly bitter again.

'It is easy to say that. If you had known about my scar, you might not have asked me to dance.'

To her surprise, Johann burst out laughing.

'That is very funny joke. I ask you to dance only because you are so good dancer. I watch you with the older man and I tell myself — Johann, here is partner for you. This is all I am caring about. You can be very old, very ugliest woman in the world, but I still wish to dance with you. But you are not ugliest old woman if you will permit me to say.'

She did not know whether to laugh or cry. At least now she knew where she stood with this strange new friend. He was interested only in her dancing. Well, that was entirely satisfactory to her. She did not want to become emotionally involved with anyone. But she loved dancing herself and now Bobbie had found a partner, it would be more amusing for her to have a partner, too, than to spend the evenings alone in her room or in the lounge reading a book.

'Are you angry with me?'

She met his anxious gaze and smiled.

'But of course not. Why should I be? I am very happy that you enjoy dancing with me. I like dancing with you, too. You are Austrian?'

'Yes, from Vienna. I have dancing four years learned in Vienna. I have taught dancing and also gymnastic, swimming and of course, ski-ing.'

'You're a ski instructor?' Sally asked.

'Of course. That is why I am living here in Zürs.'

'You take classes?'

'Sometimes. Mostly I give private ski instructions. This is very costly for people but there are many rich people come to Zürs. I will make much money here and become rich also.'

Sally felt a twinge of disappointment. Somehow it detracted from this young man's charm that he should be so materially minded.

'Is it so important to be rich?' she asked. 'Money does not buy happiness, does it?'

'Does it not? If I had been rich man, I would now be husband of girl I loved. Instead, she is married to someone else because she does not want to be poor.'

His voice was not bitter — merely matter of fact. His story was no concern of hers and yet she felt impelled to argue with him.

'Surely you are better off without her? If she had really loved you . . . '

'Ah, yes, this I tell myself often. But it does not stop me feeling lonely.'

Yes, thought Sally. Your position and mine are not so different. I know Mike didn't really love me, yet it does not stop me being, as Johann puts it, lonely all the time for him.

'Come, Sally. Is another Viennese waltz. You will dance, yes?'

She stayed dancing with him until the band ceased playing at seven o'clock. Johann accompanied her back to her table where she introduced him to the Australians and to Bobbie and Basil.

Johann bowed politely to everyone and addressing himself to Melville, whom he obviously thought to be in charge of the girls, said:

'You will please permit that I dance again with Sally this night? Is quieter here at night.'

Melville raised his eyebrows at Sally as he tried to keep a straight face. Sally nodded and Melville told Johann they would be pleased to see him later. Bobbie was on tiptoe with excitement. As soon as they reached the privacy of their bedroom, she burst out:

'I told you that guy on the bus liked you, Sal. Now we've both found someone nice. Basil's fun, but he isn't nearly as good-looking as your Johann. I'm sure he fancies you.'

Sally sat down on the bed and looked at her friend with thoughtful eyes.

'He's still in love with a girl who married someone else,' she said. 'So stop match-making, Bobbie. He's a dancing fanatic and the only interest I have for him is that he thinks I dance well. And as I love dancing, too, that's very satisfactory all round.'

'All right!' said Bobbie, dancing round the bed as she flung off her clothes to change for dinner. 'So he doesn't like you. Of course he likes you, stupid. And what's more, you like him.'

Sally sighed.

'Have it your own way. I like him . . . but that's all, Bobbie. Now hurry up or I'll bag first bath.'

While Bobbie splashed and chattered in the bathroom, Sally lay on her bed in her dressing-gown, her green eyes narrowed and thoughtful. Johann seemed nice enough. He was young,

attractive, charming, beautifully man-
nered, sympathetic — in fact, everything
a girl could want — unless the girl was
Sally Marsden and still in love with
Mike.

3

Sally dressed with more than her usual attention to detail. She wore a shocking pink polo-necked sleeveless cashmere jersey over matching slacks — an après-ski outfit she had bought in the London sales and imagined she would never have the nerve to wear. It was, because of its vivid colour, attention attracting, and she felt she had been crazy to buy it. It was something she would have adored wearing before the accident. At the last moment, she had been persuaded by Bobbie to pack it 'just in case'. Now she was actually wearing it, she felt a mixture of pleasure and nervousness.

'It's terrific!' Bobbie said breathlessly. 'You've really no idea how absolutely gorgeous you look, Sal. I just wish I had your figure and your colouring. You can thank your lucky stars you aren't redheaded and freckled like me.'

'You really don't think it's over-the-top?' Sally asked anxiously.

'No, I don't — not here. It's just perfect, Sal. Aren't you glad you brought it with you?'

But Bobbie, in her simple, enthusiastic way, had no idea what mental courage it required of her friend to go down in the lift to join the Australians for dinner. Sally kept her head high from sheer habit and training, but her eyes were on her hands which nervously clutched at a pink chiffon handkerchief which matched the chiffon turban tied round her head. She was unaware of the many admiring glances from the other hotel guests. Not even Jean's and Melville's compliments could stop the growing feeling that everyone was staring at her and wondering about that unusual turban; maybe even noticing the scar.

Her nerve had almost completely gone by the time they had finished their meal and drunk their coffee in the lounge. She no longer wished to go downstairs for the dancing which began at half past nine. She felt exhausted from the tension inside her, and when the Australian couple said they would only look in for one dance and retire early as they were tired, she eagerly agreed. She knew Johann did not live in the hotel, and wondered now if he would come to the dancing as he had promised. She had all but convinced herself he would not appear when he approached their table and asked her to dance.

As they moved on to the floor — far less crowded and quieter than it had been at tea-time — Sally began to explain that she was tired and was shortly going to leave. But before she could finish her explanation, Johann broke in:

'Is better not to talk when we dance. Afterwards we talk. Yes?'

Gradually the tension and nervousness left her. Her companion was so totally dedicated to the music and movement, she found herself following his lead and forgetting herself and her confusion and worries. His unawareness of her was strangely relaxing. She did not have to stay on her guard — to worry in case the turban was slipping from her soft fair hair and revealing the scar. She could devote herself, as he was doing, to the pleasure of dancing with a perfect partner.

When the music stopped, he looked down at her with a smile of recognition.

'Is perfect, no? We dance as one person. For me this is very great pleasure. I hope for you also?'

Sally smiled.

'Yes, indeed.' Shyly she added: 'Will you join us at our table?'

Johann thanked her and they rejoined the Tompsons, who at once burst into congratulations.

'It's a real pleasure to watch you two!' Melville said. 'You're the best dancers I've seen in ages.'

'You look as if you've been dancing together for years!' Jean commented.

'By the way, Bobbie has gone across to the Alpenhof next door with Basil. Apparently they have a disco there in the evenings. She hoped you wouldn't mind.'

Melville asked Johann what he wanted to drink and he asked for a beer.

'I must keep a clear head!' Johann explained. 'I have to give ski instruction from nine in the morning until four in the afternoon tomorrow and this I cannot do if I have drinked too much.'

The talk turned to ski-ing. Johann turned to Sally.

'If you will permit, I will be happy to give you the lesson tomorrow — but I am regretting it must be after four o'clock. You will be good skier. I shall be happy to learn you.'

Sally sighed.

'I'd be very happy for you to teach me,' she said genuinely, 'but I can't afford private lessons, much as I would like them. But thank you for suggesting it.'

Johann put down his glass of beer and looked at her with a frown. He said coldly:

'I do not wish for you to pay me. I wish that you have the lesson from me because you give me so much the pleasure with dancing.'

'Fair exchange, eh?' Melville laughed. But Sally flushed.

'No, it's not. I get as much pleasure from dancing with Johann as he does with me. He has no need to repay anything at all.'

Johann looked at her with bewilderment.

'Please, I do not understand. You are now angry?'

'Come off it, Sally!' Jean said, nudging Sally beneath the table. 'You'll only offend him if you refuse. He wants to teach you, so why not? I'd jump at the chance if I were you.'

Sally sighed. She seemed to have lost control of the situation. Everything was happening too fast. She had intended to stay uninvolved, instead she was being drawn into events against her will.

'Is now the rumba!' Johann said, getting to his feet with unusual grace in a man so tall. 'Please? You permit?'

'I can't rumba!' Sally said, but Johann merely shrugged his shoulders.

'Is not important you not know how. I lead, you follow!'

'Go on, Sally,' the Tompsons encouraged her. Once again, she could not think of a reason to refuse. She stood up and the Tompsons with her.

'We're off to bed. Enjoy yourselves!' Melville said, winking.

'I will take good care of her!' Johann said gravely, bowing to Melville and raising Jean's hand to his lips in Continental fashion. His manners were almost old-fashioned, yet somehow from him they did not seem in the least out of place.

For two hours, they danced almost every dance. In the intervals, Johann told her a little about himself. His parents had both been killed in an avalanche when he was ten and his grandmother had sent him to a school in Switzerland for five years where he had learned several languages. He had finally returned to Vienna to live with his grandmother and finish his education. When he left school he had gone to work on the railway and would have stayed in this occupation had it not been for the girl he wanted to marry. She was dissatisfied with the slow promotion and would not marry him on his existing salary. For five years he had tried to save what he could, but it was still not enough to satisfy his girl, and she had finally left him to marry a much older man who was earning twice as much in banking.

'That was when my whole life changed!' said Johann. 'I felt very bitter; very hurt and angry. I had a friend who was ski instructor and making much money. I decide I will pass my exams for instructor and do as my friend. Then when I meet again this girl I have loved, I will be richer than the man she marry and she will be sorry.'

'So you did it for revenge?' Sally asked.

Johann nodded.

'Now I have much money saved and I have good job for many more years. It is strange that I do not think much about this girl now. She is not much important to me any more. Some time I think I am thankful she treated me so. It has given me new life I like very much. I do not love again any girl I know, and this good, but soon I must marry even if I do not love.'

'Must?' Sally echoed, intrigued. 'But why?'

'Because I have great liking for the little children. I desire to have many children and soon I am too old to be young with my family. So I look now for suitable wife.'

Sally sighed.

'I don't think you can have a happy marriage that way, Johann. Surely it is important to love one's life partner? From all accounts, marriage is difficult enough even with love.'

Johann shrugged his shoulders.

'For me, it is not possible to love again. Perhaps is difficult for you to understand. I am growing up with no mother, no father. When I meet this girl, she is everything to me. I think I am also everything to her. It was not so. I am the terribly unhappy person. I wish never to feel like this no more.'

Suddenly, Sally found herself telling Johann about Mike. She knew only too well how he felt for her own experience was not so dissimilar. The recounting of her own unhappiness brought unshed tears to her eyes. His pity or sympathy might have reduced her to crying, but he offered neither. Philosophically, he shrugged his shoulders and said:

'Is very stupid man. Faces is not mattering. What is mattering is here!' He put his hand in a simple unaffected gesture against his heart.

Sally felt as if an enormous weight had been lifted from her mind. Those few simple words were really the crux of her bitterness. Johann was right.

What should have mattered to Mike was that she loved him, needed him, wanted him. If he had loved her, the scarring of her face should not have mattered. She had felt a failure ever since they split up. Now this young Austrian had made her feel that the failure was Mike's, not hers.

'I think it time you went to your sleep!' Johann broke in on her thoughts. 'I like very much to dance more but I see that you are tired. Is very high here in Zürs and new people need a little time to accustom to the air. Is also your first day of arrival. We have much time to dance more tomorrow and next day. I think is better for you to sleep now.'

Sally was touched by his thoughtfulness. She *was* tired — despite her sleep on the balcony this afternoon. So much had happened in so short a while. She could hardly believe that only forty-eight hours ago, she and Bobbie had been in their little London flat packing.

Johann escorted her upstairs to the ground floor and held open the lift door for her. As he had done with Jean, he kissed the back of her hand.

'I will look for you by the ski-lift at four o'clock,' he said. 'Perhaps is good thing for you to join in beginners' class in the morning. Then you learn to feel the skis — to stand up, turn round. This way we make more progress later.'

It was on the tip of Sally's tongue to say that she had not yet agreed to accept his offer, but the words remained unspoken. He intended to be kind and she would welcome the lesson. If ski-ing was akin to dancing and Johann had promised it was twenty times better, then she wanted to learn.

Johann suddenly reached up his hand and touched the scarf round her head.

'Is not necessary to wear this!' he said quietly. 'Is not upsetting to me to see your face, and I think happier for you, too, that you forget it.'

Before she could reply he took a step backwards and the lift door swung to between them. Automatically Sally pressed the button for the fourth floor.

As the lift rose she stood looking at herself in the mirror that covered one wall. Slowly, pensively, she pulled the chiffon scarf from her head and shook out her long, fair hair. She knew then that no matter what it cost her, she would not cover the scar again.

4

The days began to settle into a pattern. Bobbie was rarely to be seen. She spent all day in her ski class with Basil and nearly every evening at the adjoining hotel dancing with him. Sally only saw her at the tea-dance in their own hotel and at meal-times. When she came in at two in the morning, Sally was usually fast asleep.

Sally's own day was not very different. She had followed Johann's suggestion and joined the beginners' class but only for the morning. The afternoon she spent on her balcony sunbathing, and at four o'clock she had her private lesson with Johann. The tea-dance and evenings they spent either alone or with Jean and Melville.

Her ski-ing was progressing so well that Johann told her he thought she might well go up a class at the end of the week. Bobbie was not in the least put out that she was advancing much more slowly.

'I'd rather stay down in this class with Basil!' she told Sally grinning.

Basil, a tall thin dark boy, seemed as taken with Bobbie as she was with him.

'We're not really *serious!*' Bobbie told Sally confidentially, 'but we're having loads of fun. He lives in Newcastle, so I don't suppose I'll see him when we get back to England, but in a way that makes this holiday more exciting — you know, Sal — a kind of shipboard romance.'

Sally attempted to think of her own growing friendship with Johann in the same way, but she knew it was not the same. There was no question of any kind of romance between them. Johann's manner, always considerate, friendly, courteous and kind, was never anything more. Their dancing, too, was no more than a shared love for what they both did so well. Although Bobbie liked to tease Sally — and the

Tompsons, too, upon occasions — Sally was perfectly well aware that Johann's feelings were entirely platonic, as were her own towards him.

The more she grew to know him, the better she liked him. He talked of little else but ski-ing during their lessons, and only of dancing while they danced, but between whiles, they exchanged confidences about their lives in a way Sally, always reserved and what Aunt Margaret chose to call introverted, would never have believed possible. But then she had never before experienced the pleasure of a platonic friendship with a man. Her good looks had prevented this in the days before she'd known Mike and after Mike . . . well, she'd dropped all her former boyfriends without a second thought. Now she realised the satisfaction of having a man for a friend. She knew that she would miss him when she went back to England — that it might be hard to retire back into the shell which was her everyday life at home now. After the good time she was having in Zürs, the evenings alone in the flat were going to seem endless.

'But you will not go back to that life!' Johann said with conviction. 'Already you forget for many hours that you have the hurt face. Now that you have catched the sun so well, it does not nearly so much show. You will start the new life when you go home, I think.'

Sally wasn't sure. It was one thing to lose her terrible complex when she had Johann to escort her. She was very much aware of the envy of the other single girls in the hotel and on the ski-slopes. Johann was extremely good-looking and could have chosen any girl he wanted. The fact that he preferred her company flattered and bolstered her self-esteem. She could keep her head high and even at times meet the curious glances that were cast at her without being flung back into a state of depression and self-consciousness. After all, if Johann did not mind, why should she? And, as Johann said, the scar

66

showed much less now that she was tanned a lovely dark golden colour.

She wrote home to Aunt Margaret describing her life in the happiest terms. She was feeling well, eating well. She was ski mad; dance mad. She was happy.

The words flowed from her pen as she sat in the lounge, skipping the tea-dance on this her fifth afternoon at the Edelweiss, because Johann had said he had to go down to Lengen and could not attend. From where she sat she could see the reception desk. From time to time, other guests in the hotel came in, some, whose faces were familiar, nodding to her, others she thought must be new arrivals.

Suddenly her attention was caught by the woman now standing with her back to Sally as she spoke to the receptionist. She was wearing a beautiful leather jacket over tight black ski-trousers with knee-length boots of the same colour as her jacket, covering long slim legs. She was very chic and Sally's experienced eye noticed this enviously. Then the girl turned her head slightly and Sally caught her breath. It was Jess. There could be no doubt about it. The girl had the same raven dark hair, slanting eyes and *retroussé* nose. She obviously did not see Sally half hidden behind one of the tall marble pillars.

Sally looked from Jess to the lift door just behind her. If she tried to escape upstairs, Jess could not possibly avoid seeing her. Since the last thing Sally wanted was to talk to Jess, she knew she would do better to stay quietly at her table and hope that the other girl was only in the hotel to make some enquiries and would shortly leave.

But the sight of Mike's new model was not the only shock in store for Sally. As she sat, stiff and trembling slightly in her chair, Mike himself joined Jess at the reception desk.

'The dance doesn't start till five, Mike. Let's have a drink while we're waiting.'

Sally had not seen Mike since the day

he had left her in hospital — months ago now. He had not changed except that his hair was perhaps a little shorter — his face a little more sunburned than she had remembered. She wanted to avert her eyes but she could not. She was too dangerously hungry for this frightening and totally unlooked-for sight of him. He, too, was in ski-gear — caramel-coloured trousers and jersey over a black polo-necked sweater. The clothes looked perfect on his rather narrow, boyish figure.

As Sally watched he linked his arm in Jess's and they began to move towards the lounge.

Hurriedly, Sally shrank back into the depth of her armchair. Her thoughts were in chaos. She longed to get away and yet knew that this sight of Mike was like a drink of cold water to someone dying of thirst. All the old remembered pain of their loving, their parting, was as fresh and unbearable as ever. She still loved him. The sight of him coming towards her with Jess clinging to his arm, so cool, so poised, so lovely, was like the stab of a knife in her heart.

As unobtrusively as she could, she turned in her chair so that her face was averted as they passed by her, making for the little bar in the corner of the lounge. They were close enough for her to hear Jess say:

'The hotel's not nearly as smart as ours, darling!'

She bent her head over her writing pad, her thoughts chasing each other in a turmoil through her brain. What could they be doing here in Zürs?

Her postcard could not possibly have reached him, and even if it had, it did not give the name of her hotel. There were quite a number of hotels in Zürs. She would be crazy to imagine even for one moment that Mike wanted to see her enough to travel all this distance. For all those weeks and months in London he had only to telephone Aunt Margaret to discover her London telephone number if he had regretted their parting. He had never done so.

And there was Jess. It must be obvious to anyone seeing them together that Jess was now his girl.

Suddenly, Sally recalled a remark from Bobbie as she read her *Daily Express* while they breakfasted in bed. There had been a smart new English boutique opened in St Anton. (That was only half an hour away). A number of model girls had been flown out for the opening which had been a great success and created much interest with the accent on mini-skirts and cut-away dresses for evening wear.

At the time Sally had wondered if she knew any of the girls who had been lucky enough to go on the trip — but it had never crossed her mind Jess might be one of them. Still less had it crossed her mind that Mike might have gone, too, to take photographs.

But even if the opening of the boutique explained their presence in St Anton, why should Mike and Jess be here, in Zürs? As far as Sally knew,

Mike had never done any ski-ing before. He was very much a non-sporting person, London born and bred, and someone for whom the day began after mid-day and really only came alive at night. It was one of the few disagreements between them, for Sally had been brought up in Sussex and loved the country, the open air, walking, gardening . . .

'I have after all not gone to Lengen!' said Johann, his voice at her side making her jump nervously. 'There is forecast of snow, and if this should come, then the road to Lengen will of sureness be closed. Is always so. If you would like, Sally, we may go down to the dance after all?'

'Oh, Johann, sit down. I have something to tell you. I can't go down with you — not this evening!' The words came pouring out of her in a breathless rush. 'Don't look round, but up at the bar you can probably see a very beautiful dark girl with a young man — that's Mike! The one I told you about.'

Johann did not turn his head at once. His eyes remained fixed on Sally's flushed, unhappy face.

'If it is true, then is still no reason why we cannot dance if it is what you like to do,' he said calmly.

Sally clutched his arm.

'You don't understand, Johann. *They're* going dancing. That's why they are here in this hotel. They don't live here. They're probably at the Zürshof or the Lesenhauser. They'll be dancing downstairs.'

Johann covered the hand on his arm with his own cool, steady fingers.

'Calm yourself, Sally. Because this man is there is still no reason why you cannot also be there. Sometime you will have to meet again, so why not now? I will tell you — we shall dance our very most beautiful and he will watch and think to himself what silly man he is ever to leave you. How is that?'

Despite herself, Sally smiled.

'Oh, you can joke about it, Johann, but I *don't want to see him*. Don't you understand? We'd both be terribly embarrassed. He's here with Jess, and . . . '

'You are here with me. We will play little game. We will dance as two very close lovers. Perhaps even I may kiss you when it is very sentimental song like 'Spanish Eyes'. Then shall he be very sorry that he is not me.'

Sally drew a deep breath.

'You think I want to make him sorry, Johann, but I don't. I just don't want to reopen the old wounds. Just seeing him . . . knowing he's here . . . oh, please try to understand. I still love him. I've never stopped loving him.'

Now Johann's grey eyes dropped. He frowned slightly.

'This I know, but also I know it is not good thing to run away. Someday you will have to learn that you do not love him. Is better to learn this soon than late, no? You wait long time through the years and suddenly it is too late, like me, and even if you wish, you cannot love new person. That is bad. I do not wish this for you. Now I will look at this man I do not think I am very much going to like.'

She dared not watch him as he turned his head and stared for a full two minutes at the couple sitting on bar stools beside each other. When he turned back to her, she saw with surprise that his eyes were full of laughter.

'Why you not tell me he is *little* man?' he asked.

'Little man?' Sally echoed stupidly.

'Yes! Is very short man — not tall like me. Easily I can knock him on the floor if I wish.'

Now Sally was smiling again.

'I don't want you to knock him down for me, Johann. I think you are talking nonsense just to make me laugh.'

She could not be sure if there was teasing in his grey eyes, but there was certainly a twitch at the corner of his mouth.

'I think is good, my plan. Come. You will be brave and descend to the dancing with me. Is gone five o'clock and we must not waste the good hours we have. I am happy that the snow comes for I would like much better the tea-dance with you than to go to Lengen. Is only perhaps pity if still it snows tomorrow and I cannot give you ski lesson. You come with me now, Sally.'

He stood up and silently held out his hand. She knew that she could not remain seated without drawing attention in their direction. If Mike or Jess should by chance be watching, they must surely have recognised her by now.

Careful to avoid looking towards the bar, she placed her hand in Johann's and allowed him to draw her to her feet. To her surprise, he at once put an arm round her shoulders and keeping it there in a gesture that could only be called intimate, he walked her unhurriedly out of the lounge.

When they reached the stairs leading down below ground, he took his arm away and said gently:

'There! It was easy done, no? Like the stem turn — more easy when you have someone to show you . . . a good instructor like me. With me you do not have to be afraid — not of snow or of English man. I take care of my pupil, yes?'

Sally drew a deep breath.

'All right, Johann — thank you. Maybe I can face him after all — with your help. But at least let me go up to my room and fetch my scarf. Please, Johann . . . ?'

Gently, he drew her hand away from her scarred cheek.

'I wish to do most what I can to please you, Sally, but to this I must say no. It is like the ski — if bad habit begin, then it take much more long to put it right. You have not the scarf worn since three days, and I am not happy that you should feel it good thing now.'

'But, Johann . . . ' They were standing outside the room where the dancing had already started. The band was playing 'Edelweiss', a waltz Johann loved. He was already urging her through the door towards the dance floor. Suddenly, she felt the last of her resistance leave her. What did the scarf matter? What if Mike did see the scar again? Why should it matter to her when he had stopped loving or wanting her? It was only her pride — nothing but stupid pride and a feminine desire to be able to meet Jess on equal terms.

Sally did not see Mike and Jess come into the room, but she realised they must have done so when she felt Johann's arm tighten around her; heard him say:

'Put your head against my shoulder, Sally!'

Tall as she was, he was still too tall for her to dance cheek to cheek with him. Obediently she placed her cheek against the rough wool of his pullover. His steps slowed, and she felt the warmth of his body along the length of her own. Dancing like this, close to him, in some strange way his body became a refuge, a hiding place. Yet at the same time the unfamiliarity of his proximity left her nervous, caused her once or twice to miss a step and stumble slightly.

Their dancing had now reached a point where, if she put a foot wrong, Johann would gently chide her; tell her where she had gone wrong and repeat the step until she had it perfectly. But now he made no reference to her mistakes, as if he understood exactly why she faltered.

She kept her face hidden until the music stopped. Only then did she lift her head and as she looked up, opening her eyes, she found herself staring straight at Mike.

'Sally! I *thought* it was you. How fantastic! I can't believe it. You know Jess, don't you? But, of course, how silly of me!'

Sally knew every timbre of his voice; guessed that he was nervous because it was unlike him to talk in jerky abrupt sentences. Somehow, she managed a smile and a casual nod to Jess. Then she introduced Johann.

'I'm afraid my German isn't up to pronouncing Johann's surname!' she said with a short laugh. 'You'll have to say it for me, Johann!'

'You're here on holiday?' Mike was asking as the four of them began to walk off the dance floor. He had given only the most casual glance at Johann and now seemed to be ignoring him.

'Yes! And you?'

Mike explained that he and Jess had been at the opening of the boutique at St Anton; that they had decided to spend a weekend in Zürs before returning to London.

'You have come for the ski-ing?' Johann asked politely.

'Oh, no, we don't either of us ski!' Mike said. 'Just for a rest and a change. We've got rooms at the Zürshof but it's rather stuffy there — we were told it was better here at tea-time. I say, Sally, I'd no idea you were a ski enthusiast. Or are you just on holiday for the sun? You're fabulously brown!'

80

The four of them were grouped now round Mike's table. He pulled two vacant chairs from a neighbouring table and invited Johann and Sally to join them. Unfortunately Sally and Johann had not yet had a chance to reserve a table, and as the room was overflowing with people, they had no option but to take the chairs Mike offered.

Jess, her dark expressive eyes narrowed and amused, was looking up at Johann with interest.

'You are German?' she was asking.

'No, *fräulein* — Austrian!' Johann replied smoothly, although Sally knew that he did not care to be mistaken for a German, and had told her it made him very angry when anyone made this mistake.

'I thought you danced too well for an Englishman!' Jess was saying provocatively. 'Unfortunately the art is overlooked in English schools.'

Mike now looked annoyed.

'You said you liked dancing with me, Jess.'

81

'What we do isn't really dancing, is it?' Jess argued. 'Still, darling, I'd rather smooch with you than dance with anyone else!'

Her tone placating and, Sally thought with a sudden violent surge of jealousy, possessive. She knew it was stupid to care. Obviously if Mike and Jess were here for the weekend at a hotel together, it was not exactly a platonic relationship. None knew better than she the violent passionate needs that were Mike's. The only unhappiness that had marred their years together had been Mike's unrelenting efforts to get Sally to sleep with him and her own equally determined resistance. She wanted him as passionately as he wanted her — but stronger even than the satisfaction of their joint desire had been her mental determination to remain a virgin until she married. So many of their friends were living together; were happy for a while, and then one or other of the couple began to regret the association. So often, the beautiful love became a rather sordid affair. She did not want that for herself and Mike.

She knew that Mike and most of her friends, with the exclusion of Bobbie, thought she was old-fashioned, prudish, stupid. Perhaps she had been proved stupid, for Mike had allowed her to break off their relationship and, as one of her less thoughtful friends had pointed out to Sally, maybe he wouldn't have been so willing to leave her if she'd been sleeping with him. She'd thought about it often — asking herself again and again if Mike would have loved her more if they had been lovers. She would never know, and it was too late for her to find out. But it hurt her terribly to think that he and Jess . . .

'Despite Jess's rude remarks about my dancing, I hope you'll have this one with me, Sally. Remember the tune? One of our old favourites.'

They were playing Chris de Burgh's 'Lady in Red'. The tune at once transported Sally back to the penthouse where Mike had rolled back the carpet so that they could dance to his new record. They had so nearly ended that afternoon in bed together. In the end, Sally had all but run away, knowing that if she stayed in Mike's arms a moment longer, she would be unable to go on saying 'No!'

'I'm a bit tired, Mike . . . ' She tried to excuse herself now, but he refused to be put off. He covered her hand with his.

'Come on. We just *have* to dance this one, anyway!'

Sally shot Johann a quick desperate glance. He was watching her face and interpreted her look with surprising sensitivity.

'Sally injured her ankle with the skis this morning,' he said smoothly. 'She had just told me that she could not continue the dance because it was giving her some pain. If she is to ski tomorrow, I think it is better she rests her foot.'

Mike's handsome face tightened in annoyance.

'Surely Sally is the best judge of that!'

he said with barely concealed rudeness.

'Johann is my ski instructor,' Sally broke in quickly. 'I have to do exactly as he says or he won't teach me. He's a terrible bully. But I have to admit that I'm learning fast. I'm sorry, Mike. Why not dance it with Jess?'

Jess was already on her feet, her hand lying possessively on Mike's arm. He had no alternative but to take her on to the floor.

'And how is your ankle now, Sally?'

She turned her eyes from Mike and looked into Johann's laughing face.

'Better!' she said with an answering smile. But both knew that her hands were trembling; both knew that she longed with all her heart to be there on the floor with Mike's arms around her. But she could not trust herself to be there.

'Is a pity!' Johann said, holding her hand between his own and rubbing the knuckles gently, soothingly, with his cool fingers. 'Is pity because I like very much to dance this tune with you. But tonight we shall dance. I take you to little place I know. Is very nice, and you like very much. Your friends will not know, so we can forget the ankle. You like that, Sally?'

With an effort she smiled up at him. 'Yes, I like that very much!'

5

The two girls were changing for dinner. Bobbie kept glancing anxiously at Sally's serious, thoughtful face.

'I think it's rotten bad luck Mike turning up *here!*' she said, dabbing powder on her freckles. 'You were so happy, Sal! Now you're as nervous as a kitten again. I could shoot him.'

Sally put her hairbrush back on the dressing-table and let her hands drop to her lap.

'I'm all right, Bobbie. Stop worrying. I don't suppose I'll see him again. They aren't staying at this hotel, so there's no reason why we should meet.'

'But you said Mike wanted to make up a foursome here this evening after dinner!' Bobbie protested.

'Yes! But I don't think he really wanted to — he was just being polite. Anyway, I told him I wouldn't be here

— that I was going out with Johann.'

'Good for you!' Bobbie said. 'I've never said this before, but I think Mike's behaviour towards you was absolutely rotten. If I were you, I'd never want to speak to him again. How you can still be in love with him, I just don't know.'

Sally sighed.

'That's because you've never really been in love, Bobbie. It isn't something you can switch off and on at will. I don't think it would make any difference what he said or did — I'd still love him. I suppose that shocks you. You think I should have more pride.'

'So you should!' Bobbie burst out indignantly.

'Well, I can pretend I don't care outwardly — but it doesn't stop me caring inside!' Sally said quietly. 'I'd give my right arm to be Jess — here in Zürs alone with Mike. I'm so jealous I can't think of anything else. I keep wondering if he's in love with her; if they are going to be married. She wasn't wearing a ring, but . . . '

'Sal, stop it! You *can't* still want him — not after the way he treated you.'

'You don't understand Mike!' Sally broke in quietly. 'He couldn't help what happened. He blamed himself for the accident, and I was a constant reminder every time he saw me of what he'd done to me. I made him feel guilty, uncomfortable. No man wants to feel that way. And he wasn't the one to break off the engagement — I was. It wasn't even he who wanted Jess to replace me — I suggested it. I'm to blame. I practically threw him into her arms.'

Bobbie banged the wardrobe door shut, her eyes angry.

'But he didn't have to go if he didn't want to. It was such a terrible thing to do, Sal — to leave you *like that*. No wonder you were so bitter and hurt. What gets me is that you were just beginning to get over it and he has to throw you right back by turning up here like a bad penny. Perhaps you don't realise it, but Johann is the first man you've spoken to since Mike. You've been a different person these last few days — laughing, happy — how you used to be, in fact. You even stopped wearing that horrid turban thing. Oh, Sal . . . '

Impulsively she threw her arms round her friend and hugged her.

'Can't you forget he is here? Forget him — and Jess? I just hate to see you looking so miserable — especially when I'm so happy myself.'

With a great effort Sally managed to smile.

'I'm not miserable, Bobbie. You're imagining it. As a matter of fact, I'm going dancing tonight to some place Johann knows, and I'm very much looking forward to it. As to how I feel about Mike — well, I long ago stopped hoping it would all come right in the end. It was only the unexpected shock of seeing him again that threw me off balance for a little while. I'm perfectly okay now.'

'Sure?' Bobbie asked doubtfully.

'Of course I'm sure. Mike said they were only in Zürs for the weekend. That leaves only tomorrow, Sunday, and they'll be gone. I certainly don't intend to let either of them spoil my last week here.'

Bobbie relaxed and smiled.

'I'm so relieved to hear you say that, Sal. You know, I'm sure that judge knew just what he was about when he recommended you should have a really good holiday. Just look at yourself in the glass. You've lost that drawn, tense look, Sal. You're a new person — or rather, your old self again. Even the scar seems to have become almost unnoticeable.'

Sally studied her reflection. Bobbie was right. She did look well. After so many months of turning away from her mirror in horror, she could now face herself and the scar with the beginnings of approval. One more operation, to hide the slight puckering near her chin and the surgeon had promised all trace of the accident would be gone for ever.

It was at last possible to believe in this miracle. Until now she had never been able to quell the doubts that so often tormented her. The surgeon might have made those promises in order not to discourage her. Aunt Margaret, too, might have lied to keep her spirits hopeful. But what neither the surgeon nor her aunt nor Bobby could realise was that the regaining of her former good looks meant practically nothing to her since Mike had gone out of her life. It was only for him her beauty had mattered. Just as her success as a model had been important to her because it was important to him and to his career. She naturally would not have chosen to be plain, but she had had no particular desire to be really glamorous — not until she met Mike and had discovered how kind Nature had been to her. Through his eyes she had learned to value her beauty but never for itself — only for its potential for Mike; only because he derived such pleasure from it.

She stood up and managed another smile for Bobbie.

'Let's go down — I'm starving,' she lied. 'And it's venison on the menu — I noticed it at lunch-time.'

She linked her arm in Bobbie's and together they crossed the landing to the lift.

★ ★ ★

'You told me Sally didn't mean a thing to you any more!'

Jess's voice was high-pitched, irritable; the voice of a jealous woman, Mike sighed.

'How many more times, Jess — she doesn't. It's just a matter of being polite, reasonable. You must see that. After all, we *were* involved. I can't behave as if she were a complete stranger.'

Jess crossed one leg over the other as she sat perched at the bar in their hotel. Her dark brows were drawn down in a petulant frown.

'Okay, Mike, so you were polite this afternoon. I still don't see the necessity for going back to that hotel tonight.'

'It has nothing to do with Sally — I simply think it much more lively and amusing there. You don't have to come if you don't want to, Jess.'

'You're still in love with her!' Jess's' voice was now brittle, accusing. At her tone, Mike's expression hardened.

'That is typical of one of your gross exaggerations. I didn't think we'd come out here to quarrel, Jess.'

With an effort she controlled her voice and spoke more calmly, but still with a sharp undertone of jealousy.

'If you don't still care about Sally, I don't see why we don't get married. I understand when you first broke up that you couldn't in all decency rush into anything new. But that was months ago, Mike. You said . . . '

'Please don't let's go into all that again, Jess.' Mike finished off his whisky and nodded to the barman to give him another. 'You'll just have to accept that

I'm not really the marrying kind. It was different with Sally. I've explained a hundred times. Her aunt — Sally herself . . . well, it was always assumed we'd get married, and I was far too involved by the time I realised what was happening to be able to arrange anything of a lesser order.'

'You said you wanted to marry her — that you loved her!'

Mike shrugged.

'So I did. I changed my mind and that's all there is to it. Now I know I don't want to be tied, Jess; not to you or to anyone else. If you don't like it, you've only got to say.'

His companion's face changed subtly. It was now deliberately soft, appealing. The accusing note vanished. She put a hand on Mike's arm and squeezed it gently.

'I'm not complaining about our present arrangement. But you know I'm crazy about you, Mike. I couldn't help being just the teeniest bit jealous when I saw you with Sally. After all, you weren't entirely truthful about her face, were you? You made out to me she was hideously scarred.'

'So she was!' Mike now sounded uncertain of himself. 'I'd no idea such miracles could be wrought by plastic surgery. I saw a photograph, of course — taken after the court case, but I presumed it had been touched up — to hide that side of her face. Frankly, I was as astonished as you to see how . . . how much of her good looks she had regained.'

'Even with the scar she's beautiful!' Jess said grudgingly. 'That Austrian she was with was obviously madly attracted.'

Mike did not reply. He was not prepared to discuss his personal feelings with Jess. The moment she acquired any insight into his thoughts, she somehow managed to use her knowledge to her own advantage. In many ways Jess suited him. She was attractive, immensely photogenic and, above all, she did not have Sally's virginal qualms about sex before marriage. Moreover, she was in love with him, although of late this had become distinctly disadvantageous. She was becoming far too possessive . . . and jealous of any woman he spoke to for more than two minutes on end.

No, he was not going to let Jess know just how bowled over he had been seeing Sally again . . . a girl almost as beautiful as when he'd first known her; a golden, glowing *detached* Sally. Seeing her dancing so intimately in another man's arms had affected him in a most uncomfortable way. He had become so used to her utter and total devotion to him that he had never had cause to feel jealous. Sally had been heart and soul his girl. He'd taken it quite for granted and she had never given him cause to think otherwise.

He'd known perfectly well what their breaking up had done to her. Her aunt had written him a terrible letter, accusing him of breaking Sally's heart as well as her spirit, accusing him of cowardice, of cruelty; or irresponsibility. Mike had told himself that the silly old woman had no right to vent her ill feelings upon him. She could know nothing of the horror he felt every time he visited Sally in that hospital; of the horror he had always had even as a small boy of any kind of disfiguration or handicap. Some people might be able to override such weakness, but he knew that he never could. The Sally in the hospital bed ceased to be the girl he loved; she became a nightmare to him; a wreck of the Sally he'd adored both with his heart and his eyes. He knew every plane of her face; every detail of her bone structure; every line of her skin. He had photographed her so often that her image was permanently imprinted on his mind. The new tragically scarred face was not the same one he had loved and studied so minutely and reproduced so cleverly for other people's admiration. He'd felt his skin prickle in horror whenever he saw her. It had not been his fault that he had this physical reaction. Sally knew . . . and that's why she had offered him his freedom. He would have been wrong to refuse it . . . under the circumstances, and her aunt should have realised it too.

But all these months since he had last seen Sally, he had thought of her as her aunt had described; broken, wretched, unhappy, still desperately in love with him.

Well, he thought wryly as he finished his second whisky, the aunt had been wrong. Sally had not taken very long to recover either from the accident or her broken heart. The small scars had vanished altogether; the large one would no doubt soon be gone completely, too. His Sally was about to be reborn. She was still very young — and with her looks she should be able to pick up her modelling career easily. Her classic blonde English beauty was not a type to become dated in the way that Jess might. The oriental look was fashionable this year but could be quite unusable next . . .

Mike Chancery found himself not for the first time regretting his association with the girl beside him. Jess had filled the painful gap in his life when he left Sally, but he should have kept their relationship on a working basis only. He'd meant to do so, but he'd been lonely and Jess had been so crazy about him. It wasn't easy for a man to resist a persuasive, strong minded girl like Jess, especially when she was prepared to give herself to him without reservations . . .

He ought to have known there would be strings attached to their arrangements. No matter what Jess said in the early days about not expecting anything from him, like all women it had not taken long before she was demanding first his love and then marriage. They all wanted to tie a man down; put chains on him; shackle him. He, as much an artist as any painter or sculptor, needed to be free if he were to be able to express himself fully.

Somehow marriage to Sally had not seemed to present the same restriction. She was not possessive in her love in the way that Jess was. Nor did she make impossible demands upon him for his time and attention. It was almost as if she kept a small part of herself reserved and apart from him so that *he* had been the demanding one of the two, wanting more than she had been willing to give; wanting to touch that deep inner person he suspected lay beneath the sweet loving exterior. He had believed that he would find this second Sally when at last they were lovers. He'd tried and failed to establish this relationship with her and had been forced to accept that she would never be his outside of marriage. So he'd been prepared to accept the ties . . . until that horrible day. Even now he could not bear to remember the sick horror of the hospital outpatients. His own injuries, merely mild abrasions, cleaned, covered with strips of plaster, were mockeries of what had been done to Sally. He'd watched the ambulance men cleaning some of the blood pouring from her face; bandaging the terrible cuts to try to stem the bleeding, attaching the blood transfusion apparatus to her arm. Then, sitting in the hospital shocked and horrified, he waited for the doctors to come out of the operating theatre where they were trying to patch her up before she bled to death.

'Oh, God, don't let her die. Don't let her die!' It had been all he could think of then. Only later, when he had been told how terribly scarred she was, did he start to think: 'Don't let her be ugly!' His first sight of her had been so frightening. Her whole face was covered in snow-white bandages and only her eyes, still beautiful, still full of love for him, were visible. Some of the fear had gone. Sally reassured him. The doctors had promised that plastic surgery would put everything right in time.

His first sight of her without the bandages was a nightmare that even now, two years later, he could not forget. He had tried to hide his horror and revulsion but he'd failed. Sally had known how he felt, and after that, had tried to hide the worst side of her face from him. But they both knew the terrible scar was there.

He'd fought a hard battle with himself. He tried to overcome his own weakness — really tried hard. But when Sally finally told him she wished to finish their relationship, he'd felt nothing but relief. The visits to the hospital could end at last. He'd never have to steel himself to open her bedroom door again — to look at the ravages of the once perfect symmetry, the poetry of her beauty.

Maybe in the time since he had last seen her, he had exaggerated in his mind the damage done. Perhaps it was simply that the plastic surgeons had done a good job and were keeping their promise to restore Sally's face to its former loveliness. At any rate, seeing her this afternoon with only the one scar, lessened perhaps by her suntan or by make-up, he had been astonished to discover not only that he could look at her without the old horror, but that he could not in fact take his eyes away from her. She was once more as desirable as when he had first known her . . . perhaps even more so now that she was remote, lost to him, engrossed in some other man . . .

'You haven't said a word in ten minutes, Mike. Wake up, do!'

Jess's voice, childish, petulant, roused him from his thoughts. He wished once more that she wasn't here. If he'd been alone, he could have gone round to Sally's hotel and tried to get her alone, talk to her, discover what she was doing, thinking, feeling; perhaps even broach the question of the future . . . of whether she intended to restart her modelling career and if she would let him take some photographs. Perhaps he might get her to pose for him anyway. She looked fabulous in her ski outfit. With the right side of her profile towards the camera, against the white snow and blue sky, the colour effect would be stunning and her hair and skin the same perfect gold . . .

'I'd like another drink, Mike!'

'Not now!' he said abruptly. 'We'll have one at the Edelweiss. That is, if you still intend coming with me?'

Jess looked angrily into his white, stubborn face. She knew that it was useless to argue with him in this mood. If his mind was made up . . .

'All right, let's go!' she said, slipping down with easy grace from the bar stool.

'You're sure you want to come along?' Mike asked her.

She gave him a long steady stare.

'If you're going, then I'm going with you!' she told him. 'I certainly don't intend to be left here on my own.'

Mike shrugged his shoulders and, without bothering to link his arms in hers, followed her out of the room.

6

For a little while Sally forgot Mike as she took in her surroundings. She and Johann were sitting on a wooden bench at a bare wooden table. The room was like an inn, bare-boarded floor and rafters in which odd tufts of hay and straw were stuffed. Small as the room was, there was a tiny bar at one end and the tables where they sat were grouped around a minute square left free for dancing.

The air was thick with blue smoke. Dance music from a record player vied with the talk and laughter of the other occupants. On the wall directly in front of Sally was the stuffed head of a cow over which was the iron framework of a manger. Johann had been amused when Sally asked him anxiously if he thought it had once been a real cow.

'It is quite possible!' he said.

'But it has such a nice, gentle face!' Sally protested. 'Who could have wanted to kill and stuff it!'

'I expect it just died!' Johann told her, laughing. 'We Austrians are not cruel people, Sally. Perhaps even it was the great friend of some farmer man who wished to preserve his pet for always.'

After that, Sally could meet the cow's black long-lashed eyes with impunity.

They drank beer, danced, talked. Conversation with Johann was never difficult. He had led such an extraordinary life — had travelled to many countries. He had been to Hungary, Norway, Denmark, Sweden, Yugoslavia, Italy, Spain, Portugal. He had travelled as a student for the most part, learning the native languages as he went.

'Soon I hope to come to England so that I can learn better the English,' he told her. 'Perhaps I become ski instructor in Scotland. Perhaps I take job as sporting master at a school to teach the gymnastics and the swimming. I am not yet decided.'

'You could teach languages, too,' Sally suggested. 'I would like to learn your language, Johann. Teach me some words.'

But she found the accent difficult and her pronunciation made Johann laugh. For a little while she forgot to be unhappy. But as so often happened when she listened to the radio at home, a certain tune brought back the memory of Mike. Her thoughtful silence was not lost upon Johann. He said:

'You are thinking now about your Michael . . . ' He gave the name a curious German accent. 'You wish to be with him, Sally? You like I should take you to his hotel where maybe you see him?'

'No!' She swallowed, attempted a smile and said more gently: 'No, Johann. I don't want to see him. And I'm sure he does not wish to see me, either. I expect he is regretting he came here with Jess. Life is extraordinary, isn't it? It's such an unlikely coincidence meeting Mike out here. We both live in London and yet we haven't met since . . . since my accident.'

'Perhaps Fate is so arranging things,' Johann replied seriously. 'I am . . . how do you say? . . . believer in *Schicksal*. Is best not to fight when so things go. One must go the same way. That is why I ask if you wish to be seeing this man. Perhaps is so meant to be.'

'No, it wasn't Fate — it was just my bad luck!' Sally said ruefully. 'Let's not talk about him, Johann. Could we dance?'

But the dancing could not go on for ever. It was soon midnight and Johann paid the bill and led her out of the strange little club which was below ground level. Holding her arm, he guided her up the steps, which were snow-covered and icy. High above their heads a brilliant moon shone down from a black star-spangled sky. The air was so cold Sally gasped. Johann pulled the white fur hood of her anorak more closely around her face. Suddenly he paused, his hands holding the fur

109

beneath her chin, and looked down at her with a curious expression.

'I had not known you were so beautiful!' he said softly.

Then he kissed her.

His lips barely brushed hers before he withdrew his mouth and smiled down at her.

'You do not be sorry I did that? Please to excuse me if it was wrong.'

Startled, uncertain but not in the least sorry or angry, Sally smiled back at him.

'Come!' Johann said cheerfully. 'We walk most carefully to the hotel. We tell earlier the lie about your ankle. Is better you do not slip on the ice and make the lie come true.'

They walked now in silence. Johann's arm was firmly around her, not in intimacy but to steady her. She felt a great surge of liking for him. His consideration, his charm, his proffered friendship were so very much what she was needing. Her heart was not free to cope with anything more. Unknowingly, he had struck exactly the right note. Anything more personal and she would have stopped seeing him, going out with him. They liked each other and were friends . . . it seemed enough and satisfactory to them both.

It was not often that Johann came into the hotel with her, but tonight on an impulse she did not fully understand, she asked him if he would come in for a few minutes.

'We could get some hot coffee in the bar downstairs,' she said. 'That is, if you are not too tired?'

'This I would very much like,' he said at once.

They went through the hotel lobby and downstairs. The band was still playing in the big dance room on the right. They turned left and went into the bar. There were twenty or so people in the room which was dark and more dance music was being played softly in the background on tape.

It was a moment or two before Sally noticed Mike and Jess sitting at a corner table. Mike was already on his feet, coming towards them.

'Hullo, Sally. I came here hoping to run into you, but I'd about given up and was just leaving.'

He nodded to Johann and turned back to Sally:

'How's the ankle? Let me buy you a drink. Will you and . . . your friend . . . ' He paused with a none too friendly glance at Johann . . . 'Care to join Jess and me at our table?'

'I'm just going to bed!' Sally said, conscious now of Mike's light touch on her arm, the appeal in his eyes. 'As you can see, we're just having coffee . . . '

'I do not drink either,' said Johann. 'I must not have bad head tomorrow when I teach the ski.'

'Maybe I'll have a few lessons!' Mike looked at Sally, not Johann, as he spoke. 'Perhaps I could come with Sally if her ankle is better? How much do you charge, Johann?'

Sally saw Johann's face flush. She understood why. Something in Mike's

112

Sally went into the bathroom and began to take off her make-up with cold cream. For many months she had tried not to remember the past, but now so many little incidents were forcing their way back into her mind. There had been the trouble about Aunt Margaret. Sally adored her aunt, who was more like a mother to her than her own mother, who had died when Sally was a baby. But Mike and her aunt did not hit it off terribly well. At first Aunt Margaret had been pleased for Sally when Mike had shown such an interest in her career and had been as eager for Sally as she was for herself to make a success of her modelling. But when they fell in love, although Aunt Margaret tried not to show it, she was never at ease with Mike, and he . . . well, he quite openly said he wished Sally didn't have any relations. He resented the weekends Sally went home, and yet he had refused to go with her. He hated the country and said he was bored sitting around doing nothing. He didn't like gardening and, mostly at weekends, Sally and her aunt cared for the lovely little garden they had planted and tended with such pleasure through the years. Walking, too, was anathema to Mike, so it was only natural he was bored, and Sally understood how he felt and did not press him to come after the first few unsatisfactory visits.

'Your aunt fusses so absurdly about you!' Mike protested. 'Anyone would think you were still a child. Doesn't she realise you're a grown-up woman now, free to live your own life the way you want?'

'But I do, Mike. She never tries to stop me doing anything I want. She only fusses because she loves me . . . she wants to be sure I eat enough and don't get wet feet or go out without a coat because she cares so much about me.'

'I still think it's high time she let you off her apron strings!'

'I'm still a minor — technically she is

my guardian!' Sally argued. 'Please try to like her, Mike. She's my nearest and dearest relative and I owe her so much.'

But Mike, though he was never overtly rude, made it quite obvious to Aunt Margaret how he felt about her. If she came to the studio when he was there, he made some excuse and left. Aunt Margaret was hurt but did her best not to show it. Sally tried to explain to her that because Mike had never got along well with his own parents, he was against all relations: that it wasn't anything personal against her.

'No, it isn't that!' Aunt Margaret had said sadly. 'It's that he knows I don't trust him.'

Sally wiped the last of the cold cream from her face and began to brush her hair.

After the accident — after Mike had left her, she had waited for Aunt Margaret to say 'I told you so!' but she never did. She never mentioned Mike unless it were absolutely necessary to do so in relation to the court case. They had had only one argument about that. Aunt Margaret wanted her to sue Mike and she did not.

'He is insured, Sally. *He* won't have to pay. I'm not asking you, nor would I do so, to get damages from him.'

No, her aunt had been wonderfully understanding. She was not vindictive. If Mike knew, surely he would change his mind about her . . .

Sally put down her hairbrush and stared back at her reflection in the glass, her eyes narrowed thoughtfully. She must not start thinking this way. It didn't matter any longer whether Mike liked or understood Aunt Margaret or not. There was no question now of how often or otherwise they'd visit her when they were married; no question of whether Aunt Margaret would try to dissuade her from marrying him. The relationship was over, the romance was off; the love he'd once had for her was gone. His interest now was only a friendly one — perhaps even a relic of the guilt he'd felt. To ignore her now and not proffer a friendly interest would have been cruel, unthinkable. She must not read anything more into the situation than existed. She must not imagine the look in Mike's eyes — she obviously had only imagined that he was really anxious to be with her; even a little jealous of Johann . . .

She climbed into bed and pulled the big white feather duvet round her shoulders. She had opened the windows and the night air was bitingly cold. It was possible to see the snow-covered mountain peaks faintly outlined against the dark sky. She wondered if Bobbie had come in yet? How simple and uncomplicated Bobbie's life was compared with her own. She had masses of boyfriends at home, and now she was having an uncomplicated amusing time with Basil. Love had never yet come as a torment to Bobbie. Perhaps it never would. She was not one for very deep emotions. Maybe she would end up happily married to a man like Basil, having children, enjoying the simple things in life.

For Sally, love was over and finished with. She had known when Mike left her that she'd never love anyone else again. She could like other men. Johann had taught her that friendship with a man was not impossible for her as she had once imagined. But love . . . no! She never wanted to be vulnerable again to that torment, that heartbreak, that agony of knowing her love was not returned.

In the dark, her hands reached up and touched the scar on her face. That would go. Perhaps even the inferiority complex she'd developed about her appearance would go. Certainly since she'd been with Johann, she had begun to feel attractive again. Tonight he had told her she was beautiful — even if it was when they were standing in a very dim light outside the door! But he'd sounded quite genuine and he'd actually wanted to kiss her. Of course she hadn't minded! She was learning to look up and hold her head high. But the deeper invisible scar would never go. She could never trust a man again. She almost envied Bobbie who, with her rather plain little face and snub nose and freckles, must know that when a man said he loved her, it was for the kind of person she was and not for a beauty that could so easily be lost. Mike had loved her, Sally, for her looks. That had been the hardest part of all to bear. If he had loved the woman behind the face, no scar, however terrible, could have changed his feelings.

'I won't see him tomorrow!' she thought. 'It's too dangerous. I might start caring . . . falling in love all over again, and then . . . '

But she knew she lied to herself. She couldn't fall in love with Mike all over again because she had never stopped loving him. She had never stopped wanting him; never stopped longing for the phone to ring; for the front door to open and for him to walk in; for the postman to bring a letter from him saying he wanted to see her. She had not expected any of these things to happen, but she'd never really given up hope.

'I won't be bitter!' she thought as she turned her hot face to a cooler part of the pillow. 'I'm lucky; lucky that the accident happened and I found out about Mike before I married him. Even if there'd been no accident, one day I'd have grown old and wrinkled and he'd have stopped loving me just the same. I'm lucky I wasn't killed, paralysed, scarred far more seriously and lastingly. I'm lucky to have been given all that money by the court, to be here, to have met Johann.'

But even as she fell asleep, the thought lay in her mind — was she also lucky to have met Mike here in Zürs? Was this a second chance? Was Fate, as Johann suggested, contriving to give her Mike's love back again?

7

Johann was late. Sally sat in the lounge from where she could watch the people coming in the hotel door. It was nearly ten-thirty when eventually he arrived and came straight over to her, his face without its usual customary smile of welcome.

'I am afraid your friend has had an accident,' he said at once, sitting down beside her and removing his gloves and anorak.

'Bobbie? But she was here ten minutes ago . . . ' Sally began when Johann broke in:

'No, not Bobbie — Mike. He has fallen coming from his hotel. He has very badly sprained the ankle. I also was coming from this direction when I saw many people standing round him in the road and learned what had happened. I went myself to fetch the doctor while some others carried him back to his hotel. He has much pain, I am afraid.'

Sally's heart jolted. The thought of Mike hurt, in pain, was a shock. Johann saw her face whiten and said:

'I have thought as I came here perhaps you wish to go to the Zürshof to see him? Maybe we should not after all go to St Anton?'

Sally hesitated. She did not want to disappoint Johann and yet he had guessed very accurately how she felt. She wanted to throw on her anorak and rush round to Mike — now, at once. But she couldn't. Jess was there to look after him and the doctor would be there, too, and if Mike wanted her, he . . .

'Fräulein Marsden, you are wanted on the telephone!'

The voice of the young, friendly receptionist made Sally jump. Her heart was racing as she went into the telephone box in the hall.

'Sally? It's me — Jess! Mike has just

had a rather nasty accident — it's his ankle. He fell and sprained it.'

Jess's voice was matter of fact.

'Yes, I know. Johann just told me.' Sally forced the words out. Her heart was racing.

'The doctor at the Clinic has put it in plaster. I rang because . . . ' She paused and began again. 'Mike told me to ring and ask you if you could come round to the hotel and cheer him up. He says he's feeling pretty rotten, and . . . well, he'd like you to come.'

'I see!' There was no need for Sally to ask Jess if *she* wanted her there. It was quite clear from the cool tone of her voice that she did not.

'I was going to St Anton with Johann,' she said doubtfully.

For a moment Jess did not reply. Then she said:

'Mike said I wasn't to take no for an answer — that I was to make you come.'

Sally was acutely embarrassed. It wasn't hard to guess how poor Jess was feeling. For Mike to want her, Sally, when Jess was already with him . . .

'Tell him I can't come . . . at least, not now. Johann's just arrived. I'll try and call in for a few minutes after lunch. All right?'

'I'll tell him!' Jess said curtly, and the phone went dead.

Sally stood in the empty booth feeling the palms of her hands wet with tension. Every nerve was urging her to go. Mike had asked for her. *He wanted her, not Jess.* And she wanted to go. She would have gone now, this minute, but for Jess.

Poor Jess! Sally knew all too well what it felt like to love someone and not have that love returned. Jess must love Mike to have made that call for him. It must have needed a terrible effort. Mike ought not to have asked it of her. He should have waited until Jess was out and rung himself . . . or not rung at all.

She went slowly back to the table and told the waiting Johann about the phone call.

'What should I do, Johann? *Should* I go?'

He gave an imperceptible shrug of his shoulders.

'I cannot answer for you, Sally. You *want* to go, yes?'

'Yes, but there's Jess . . . if she loves him, perhaps I ought not to go. I don't know. I don't really know why Mike wants *me* there.'

'You are sure that this girl Jess is in love with him?'

Sally's eyes widened.

'No, I'm not sure. But I have a feeling about it. I think she does. She wouldn't be here with him if she didn't. She always did like him. Mike knew her even before he met me. I don't want to hurt her, Johann.'

'She will be already hurt, Sally!' Johann said quickly. He beckoned to one of the waitresses and ordered coffee for them both. 'I do not think if you go to visit with Mike, it will hurt her more. It is you who can be hurt. This I do not want for you.'

'You are probably right, Johann. How is it you can always see things so clearly? I suppose I'm still in love with him. You are very kind, very patient with me. I must be an awful drag. You would have liked to go to St Anton, wouldn't you?'

'Only if it pleased you — otherwise I have no pleasure to go,' he replied simply.

The coffee arrived and Sally poured out two cups and passed Johann's to him. She drank some of the hot liquid and tried to think calmly.

'Perhaps we *should* go to St Anton,' she said, more to herself than to him.

'I think we should not — not today. You cannot be always afraid, Sally. This I have learned when I was very young. It is not good, as I have told you, to run away. Go and see him. Maybe it will not make you happy but at least you will then know, is it not so?'

He made the decision sound simple. She felt that he was right, too. When she saw Mike, talked to him, if Jess were not there, she might find out how he really felt about her; if he still cared at all, if . . .

'Finish your coffee, Sally. It becomes quickly cold.'

She did as he told her and then looked at him anxiously.

'Johann, will this mean Mike can't go home tomorrow?'

'It is possible. He may have much pain for a day or two. If it is important he go, then I think it is possible, but I do not think he will wish to travel in such state.'

Sally felt a rush of confusing emotions; relief that Mike might not after all be leaving; fear because she could see all too clearly that she was becoming involved again, and once that happened, she was open to a renewal of all the old hopes, despairs, torments. It would be better for her if he went, and yet she was already alive with the anticipation that he would stay.

She looked up at Johann and suddenly saw him quite differently, not

131

as a newly acquired and pleasant acquaintance, but as a very old and dear friend; someone she could trust absolutely; important to her in a new and unaccountable way when she considered what a short time she had known him.

'You are very nice, Johann!' she said.

'Nice? It is an English word I hear often but am not so sure how is translated in my language. What does it mean, Sally?'

The blue-grey eyes were half-smiling. Sally felt herself relax.

'Oh, it means lots of things. Kind, thoughtful, sympathetic, understanding. Lots of things, Johann. I am so glad I met you. I wish . . . '

She broke off, suddenly unsure of herself.

'You wish . . . ?' Johann prompted, but she dropped her eyes and said softly:

'I don't know. I'm all confused. I think I was going to say I wish I'd always known you, but that's silly, isn't it? In a way, though, I do feel as if I'd known you for years. Why is that, Johann?'

Now it was his turn to look away. He ran his finger round the edge of his coffee cup and seemed for a moment intent upon his childish pursuit. Then he spoke, avoiding a direct reply:

'I, too, feel I have known you for a very long time. When first I have seen you in the bus coming up from Lengen, I think I have known you before. Perhaps this is because I have one time seen your picture in paper. Perhaps I only dream a face like you have.'

'That could be a nightmare, not a dream!' Sally said, half-laughing, uncomfortably self-conscious.

Johann pushed aside the coffee cups and in a more casual tone of voice, said:

'I think we have talked enough this morning. Would you like to ski a little while? We have time before lunch.'

It seemed to Sally an excellent way to pass the remainder of the morning. It would keep her mind off Mike . . . off

133

the impending visit she knew she would make that afternoon.

At lunch-time Bobbie listened to Sally's account of the accident and told Sally she was crazy.

'How many times have you told me, Sal, that you never wanted to see Mike again? That even if he did get in touch with you, you'd never be so silly as to trust him, or yourself with him, again. He'll only let you down a second time. He's not worth it, Sal. *Please* don't go!'

Sally flushed. She knew Bobbie was only speaking out for her sake, but she didn't want to listen to her friend's warnings. She said irritably:

'Don't be so dramatic, Bobbie. I'm only going to sit and chat for a few minutes. There's no question of restarting anything. Don't be stupid!'

Bobbie did not reply, but Sally could see from her expression, from the worried frown on her forehead, that she was not convinced.

When lunch was at last finished and she started the short walk from her hotel to Mike's, Sally felt her own nerve giving way. Bobbie was perfectly right — she was crazy to see any more of Mike than was absolutely necessary. She had no foundation whatever for thinking he was still in love with her; feeling as she still did about him, she could bring herself nothing but unhappiness by this visit.

But her feet took her forward, down the icy road, towards the hotel, ignoring the warnings that her brain kept giving her; ignoring the feeling that became stronger each yard she took that she should turn round and go back before it was too late.

* * *

'Sally! You look absolutely fabulous. How wonderful of you to come! I was afraid you wouldn't!'

Mike was in bed, his face turned eagerly towards her as she came in the door. He pointed to a chair beside the bed.

'Come and sit here. Jess has gone out to see if any of the shops are open. We've time for a good chat before she gets back.'

Slowly Sally went towards him. His face looked white and drawn as if he was in pain.

'How is the ankle?' she asked as she sat down beside him.

'Hurts a bit, but I'm not going to think about it now you're here. Anyway, I'm not all that sorry it happened. Now I've a good excuse to stay on in Zürs.'

His eyes were smiling directly into hers, but his voice was serious.

'An excuse?' Sally echoed nervously.

'Yes! Now I've found you out here I'm not in any hurry to get back to London. The doc said he'd give me a certificate to say I shouldn't travel tomorrow, so you see, there's no reason why I can't stay on.'

'And Jess?' The question came out before Sally could stop it.

Mike's eyes dropped. His face darkened.

'She's going home tomorrow. She wanted to stay but . . . Anyway, Sally, I think it's better if she does leave. We've been seeing a bit too much of each other lately. We do nothing but quarrel and argue. Frankly, I'll be glad when she's gone.'

Sally remained silent. She was torn with pity for Jess and yet she could not help the leap of her heart when she realised that Mike wasn't in love with Jess . . .

' . . . I never meant things to get serious,' Mike was saying as he reached out and took Sally's hand, holding it in his own. 'I'm afraid Jess got the idea somehow that our business partnership could develop into a more personal one and . . . well, I just don't want to get involved with her, nor ever did.'

Sally lifted her head and met Mike's blue intent eyes. Her whole body seemed to melt with remembered weakness that just his look could evoke in her. The weeks, months, in hospital were forgotten. She could think only of those happy times in the past, of the deep consuming love she'd felt for him.

'Sally, darling, we were crazy ever to let each other go!'

He was holding both her hands now, trying to draw her closer to him. Yet his words were so exactly the ones she'd longed to hear, she could think of little else.

He sensed her resistance and said softly, urgently:

'You can't tell me you don't care anything about me any more. Don't say I've been wrong about you. The way you avoided me yesterday, the look in your eyes . . . Sally, you do still care a little, don't you?'

Quite involuntarily, her hand went to her cheek, touched the scar. Mike's eyes followed the movements. He looked quickly away.

'You can't be so cruel as to remind me of what I did to you, Sally. Do you think I haven't lain awake at nights torturing myself with remorse? It's never been out of my mind . . . that terrible accident and what I did to you. Won't you ever forgive me?'

'Oh, Mike, *don't!*' Her defences were totally swept away now. 'You must know I don't blame you . . . I never did . . . not for the accident.'

'You mean because I left you . . . afterwards?'

She could not reply. She had not come prepared for this conversation, for any of this. She wasn't prepared to find Mike still in love with her. She'd thought only of how she felt about him.

'Sally, you wanted us to break up. You begged me to go. I didn't want to leave you. You sent me away!'

She drew her hands away, trying to stop her racing thoughts; to think calmly, unemotionally. But Mike caught her arm and pulled her fiercely down beside him.

'I didn't want to leave you, Sally. *You* made me go!'

Somehow she was quite sure in the very back of her mind that this wasn't true, but even as the thought took hold, it was swept away as unimportant. It just didn't matter now whose fault it had been that Mike had left her. The only important thing was that he hadn't wanted to go; he hadn't stopped loving her any more than she had stopped loving him. They should never, never have parted.

His face was very close to hers now. His eyes were closed as his mouth came down to hers. Then he kissed her. At the same moment, the door opened abruptly and Jess walked in. She stood in the doorway staring at them, her large dark eyes enigmatic.

'Sorry if I'm interrupting!' she said as Sally drew quickly away from Mike's embrace, her face deeply flushed. Mike looked sullen — like a small boy who had no intention of feeling repentant.

'You could have knocked!' he said coldly. The cruelty of his words struck Sally so forcibly that she drew further away and said:

'It's all right, Jess. Please come in. We — '

'I'm not staying!' Jess interrupted, her eyes flashing as she looked beyond Sally to Mike. 'I'm not the fool you take me for, Michael Chancery. Don't think your lies deceived me. I knew why you wanted Sally here. I suppose I've known for a long time you weren't in love with me. Well, more fool me for *ever* believing that you were.'

'For God's sake, Jess, let's not have another scene in front of Sally. If you're going, why not go?'

'Mike!' Sally looked from one to the other, confused and embarrassed. 'I'm the one who should leave.' She picked up her gloves but Mike at once caught her arm.

'No, I want you to stay, Sally. Jess might as well know. It's all over between us and the sooner she accepts it the better.'

'Oh, I accept it!' Jess said scornfully. 'As a matter of fact, I've about reached the end of my own tether, Mike. You don't really think being in love with you has been fun for me, do you? You're the most selfish man I think I've ever met. And the most self-opinionated. And the most cruel. Women don't really matter to you, do they? Except as playthings? I tried to tell myself you weren't responsible for the way you treated Sally. I wanted to believe the best of you, Mike — not the worst. Now I know what kind of a man you really are.'

'Get out!' Mike said furiously. 'You're so jealous of Sally you don't know what you're saying. I never said I'd marry you. I never pretended to be in love with you. You've nothing to reproach me with.'

Jess's lips curled.

'Oh, no, Mike, you never actually signed on the dotted line, did you? But you let me hope . . . and go on hoping. You let me think right up to this trip out to Austria that you did care; that eventually if I stuck around long enough . . . oh, well, the blindfold is off now. I'd wish you both luck only, despite what you say, I've never disliked

Sally and I wouldn't wish you on her now.'

She turned and gave Sally a long, penetrating look.

'Don't let him do this to you, Sally. I'm honestly not saying this because I want him myself. I love him all right, but I don't want him now I know what he's really made of. He's no good — to you, to me, to any woman. There's only one person who will ever count for anything to Mike and that's Mike. Get out while it's not too late, Sally, for your own sake.'

'She's jealous . . . she knows how I feel about you and she'll say anything to get rid of you,' Mike said furiously. 'Don't listen to her, Sally, please.'

Sally felt as if she was being torn in pieces. She wanted to believe Mike; to trust him; to be able to say with complete conviction: 'I know him, Jess. He's not as you say.' But the words would not leave her throat. Jess did not sound like a jealous woman — she sounded bitter, disillusioned.

She sounded as Sally herself had felt when Mike left *her* . . .

'I have to go now, Mike,' she said. 'Johann is waiting for me. I said I'd only be a few minutes!' The lies, once started, flowed easily. 'I'll get in touch. I hope you'll be better soon!' She pulled her arm free and without daring to look at the man in the bed, she pushed past Jess and went through the door, banging it behind her.

'Now see what you've done. I'll never forgive you for this, never,' Mike flared. 'You can get out of my life and stay out. You knew damn well how I felt about Sally. You knew I'd never stopped loving her. You just wanted to spoil my chances of getting her back.'

Jess walked over to the bed and stood looking down at Mike, her face as white and as angry as his.

'Love, Mike? You don't know the meaning of the word. Do you think a man in love would walk out on his girl just because her face was cut up? That's not love! You're only attracted now because the scars have disappeared and made her desirable again. You're the one who is jealous, Mike. You saw her with that Austrian guy and your pride was piqued. You expected her to drop into your lap a second time, didn't you? Then, when you found she had other fish to fry, you changed your tune. You don't love her, Mike. You just want her — the way you wanted me, remember?'

'Will you please go, Jess?' He was no longer looking at her. His voice sounded tired. 'You're boring me!' he added.

'Oh, I'll go!' Jess said. 'As a matter of fact I wasn't out shopping — I was packing. I'm going down to Lengen on the next bus and I'm catching the night train home, so put your mind at rest, Mike, on that score. It's Sally I'm thinking of now. And I'm warning you, I shall do anything I can think of to stop you hurting her. She's a nice kid . . . far, far too good for you.'

'Neither Sally nor I need your interference!' Mike said. 'Do your worst, Jess, but you won't succeed in coming between us. Sally still loves me. I know it and, what's more, *you* know it. She'll be back, though you won't be here to see it.'

'Nor do I wish to be. I know what you really are now, and if Sally is weak enough, fool enough, to fall for you a second time, I pity her. I was a fool ever to let myself fall in love with you. You aren't worth it. But I'll save Sally from you . . . if I can.'

Jess's eyes filled suddenly with tears. She turned quickly away before Mike could see them and without a backward glance hurried out of the room. She did not go to her own room, but went downstairs and out on to the road where Mike had had his accident earlier in the day. Her face was hard and determined as she hurried towards the Edelweiss. She knew that she must see Sally, talk to her, before she could weaken and change her mind. If she stopped to think, she might start feeling sorry for Mike, alone in that room, unable to get up and defend himself: unable to follow Sally and put his case. She might find herself starting to make excuses for him. Worst of all, she might start believing that he really had loved Sally and only Sally; that their break up had been not of his, but of her making. It was all too easy to want for Mike what he wanted for himself — easy because, despite everything she had said, she still loved him, still wanted to give him everything in the world that he desired.

8

Sally was not in the hotel lounge when Jess went in. Johann was sitting alone at the table where they had had coffee. When Jess approached him, he stood up with his usual good manners and waited for her to speak.

'Sally told me she was going to her room,' he said in reply to Jess's query as to her whereabouts. 'I think she will be down in a little while. She promised to me she would join me for the tea-dance.'

Jess sat down without waiting for an invitation. She waited until Johann, too, was seated, and looked at him speculatively.

'You're fond of Sally, aren't you?' she said abruptly.

It was Johann's turn to look at the girl opposite him, his glance uncertain. She was all but a total stranger to him.

He was surprised at her question but as if she took his reply for granted, she went on:

'If you are a friend of Sally's, you'll keep her away from Michael Chancery. She's a good kid — too nice to be hurt the way he'll hurt her. Can't you take her away from here somehow? Away from Zürs?'

Johann offered Jess a cigarette and lit it for her. He used the few moments of time to try to sum her up. Was she really Sally's friend or was she just trying to get Sally out of the way because she feared her effect on Mike?

As if in answer to his thoughts, Jess said:

'I'm leaving Zürs on the twenty to five bus so don't think I've any axe to grind. I'm just thinking of Sally.'

'This is not of my affair, I think,' Johann said quietly. 'I am only now meeting with Sally and it is not right for me to tell her how she must make her life.'

Jess leant back in her chair and blew

out a cloud of smoke. Her dark pencilled eyebrows were raised in thought.

'Forgive me if I embarrassed you. I thought . . . well, I had the idea you and Sally were . . . perhaps I was wrong. I watched you dancing together and I thought . . .'

'You were altogether not wrong,' Johann broke in impulsively. Surprisingly, he felt he could trust the girl talking to him so unexpectedly. 'I have the very deep regard for Sally. I do not wish to see her hurt. I think already has she been hurt sufficient, no? But I cannot have the right to make this my business.'

Jess leant forward, her voice steady now as she became more sure of herself and of the young Austrian she was talking to.

'I know you can't interfere directly, but if you could somehow persuade her to go? She would think, as perhaps you did a moment ago, that I wanted to keep her away from Mike for my own purpose. I give you my word it isn't so. I never want to see him again. But I'm terribly afraid Sally is still in love with him. I'm equally sure he doesn't love her. Isn't there anything you can do?'

Johann's broad shoulders shrugged imperceptibly.

'I cannot leave Zürs myself. My job is here. I can suggest to Sally that she go, but I think she would not consider it. There is the young girl, Bobbie, to remember. Also, I have told Sally that it is never no use in life to run away. If she goes home to London, can this man not follow her? If not today or tomorrow, then next day or next week or next month. If what you say about him is true, and he does not love her, Sally must discover for herself, no?'

Jess sighed.

'I suppose so. You may be right. I had not thought of it like that. I really hadn't thought it out at all. It's been such a nasty shock for me. I thought Mike really cared for me. But since he saw Sally again . . . well, he's made it quite plain he wants to drop me now he thinks he can get Sally back.'

Johann's face looked suddenly drawn and tired.

'Perhaps you are wrong, Fräulein, and he really does love her?'

Jess's mouth tightened.

'Perhaps you don't know what happened — how he walked out on her when she needed him most.'

'Yes, of this I know. Sally has not forgotten either. I trust she will remember this whenever she is with him.'

'Oh, you men!' Jess burst out involuntarily. 'You don't have any idea how blind women can be when they are in love. They don't *want* to remember the faults and the hurts and disillusionments. They refuse to face them. I know. Deep down inside I've known all along the kind of man Mike is, yet I wouldn't admit it, not to anyone and least of all to myself. It'll be the same with Sally. She'll listen to all the words she longs to hear — and Mike is so clever with words. He'll talk and talk and end up making her believe *she* walked out on *him!* If I could only make her see what he's really like underneath all the charm and the blarney.'

'Blarney?'

Suddenly Jess smiled. The sadness was gone from her face and with it the bitterness and tension.

'It means flattery, I suppose,' she told him as she picked up her purse and gloves and stood up. 'Perhaps you won't know what that means, either. I think you are probably a very honest person. I hope Sally chooses you!'

Johann's face coloured slowly. He hesitated before he said falteringly:

'I hope this also!'

Jess smiled.

'So I wasn't wrong — you *do* care. Well, good luck, and do what you can to help her, won't you? Say good-bye for me.'

Johann nodded and waited for her to leave the hotel before he sat down again, his face serious and thoughtful. He was not quite sure how such a strange conversation had come about. Ten minutes ago, he would have said he was incapable of talking to a stranger about his innermost feelings. Moreover, he had not previously admitted even to himself just how he felt about Sally Marsden. Now, because the admission had been forced from him, he knew that he was in love with her. It was stupid ever to have pretended otherwise. Since her arrival in Zürs he had had no time for anyone else. Alone at night in his room, he had been unable to sleep for remembering everything she had said; everything they had been doing together; the shared jokes and dances and conversation. He had come in for quite a bit of teasing from his fellow instructors — but then he was used to that. They all ribbed him and one another when any of them had an attractive girl pupil. They had been envious, too. Sally was a very beautiful girl — despite the scar which he,

154

himself, no longer noticed. She was also very sweet. He had thought her kind, sensitive, intelligent and quite charming. But he had not let himself think that he loved her. He had believed that he was finished with love. For two whole years after his girl had married a richer man than he, he had been hurt, bitter, disillusioned. Then he had begun to harden his heart. By degrees he had succeeded in convincing himself that no woman was worth the heartache. When he married, he would do so purely for convenience, choosing a girl who would make him a good wife and be a mother to the children he desired one day to have. In return he would offer her the security of the healthy bank balance he was steadily accruing. They would have a pleasant understanding; unemotional, sensible, reliable. Love would not come into it. Now he had been forced by a complete stranger to realise that he was not, after all, proof against love. At first, he had been only attracted by Sally's beauty, for he saw her as beautiful; and when he discovered her painful inferiority complex about her scarred face, his chivalrous instincts had been aroused and he had determined to try to restore her self-confidence. He had managed to convince himself that his interest in her was for her sake rather than for his. But last night, when he had kissed her, he had felt something quite new — a desire to hold and possess her; a need of her outside and beyond her need of him. He knew now that he had felt jealousy, too, of the man she had once loved and who was obviously trying to reclaim her. Yet his reactions had been quite the opposite of a man in love — he had all but thrown her back into Mike's arms, encouraging her to go and visit him instead of rushing her off to St Anton as now he wished he had.

He glanced at his watch and saw that it was after four o'clock; over an hour since Sally had come back, tense and white-faced, from the Zürshof. He wished now that he had persuaded her to stay down here talking to him. At least then he would have known what exactly had happened between her and this Michael. Something must surely have transpired for Jess to be leaving Zürs. Someone now would have to look after Mike. He, Johann did not wish for it to be Sally.

'I don't want her even to talk to him!' he thought with a surge of feeling so violent that it frightened him. 'I will keep her from him somehow!'

He felt his muscles tense as he recalled what Jess had said. Michael was no good to Sally. He did not love her — would hurt her again as he had already once hurt her so seriously. What was it the Englishman possessed that made him so attractive to women? Why did Sally love him? *Did* she still love him? A hundred questions surged through his mind in disorder. But out of all his self-questioning, only one salient fact emerged and that was that he, Johann, loved Sally and would do anything he could to prevent her being hurt again.

'Oh, Johann, have you been waiting for me? I'm so sorry. I thought you'd go off and come back for the tea-dance!'

Sally's remorseful voice jolted Johann from his thoughts about her. He stood up quickly and, as was his custom, kissed her hand. She smiled at him and they sat down. Johann ordered two cups of the thick sweet chocolate with whipped cream he knew Sally enjoyed.

'I have had a visitor!' he told Sally, very much aware of her pallor and the dark shadows beneath her eyes. He was afraid she might have been crying. He looked at the scar on her cheek and felt a strange pain inside himself, as if the scar were his own. He longed to touch her, to reach out a hand and hold it gently against her cheek. He wanted to tell her about his newly discovered love for her. He wanted to kiss her. Most of all, he wanted to be near her.

'It was Fräulein Jess. I do not know her other name. She wished to see you — to tell you goodbye as she is leaving Zürs this evening.'

The colour flamed in Sally's cheeks.

'So she really is going. I didn't think she would. Not with Mike . . . ' She broke off, as if afraid of what she was about to say.

'I think she has said the final goodbye to Mike. Sally, I think it would be good if you, too, would say the final goodbye.'

Sally's head jolted backwards and she looked at Johann with fire in her eyes.

'Jess has been saying things against him. You shouldn't have listened to her, Johann. She's upset, I know, but she had no right to speak against him.'

Johann's heart sank. This was a new Sally — a woman in defence of the man she loved. He could not plead with her. Why would she listen to him — a mere friend who meant nothing to her? He had no justification for interfering in her life.

His silence impressed itself on Sally. She was aware that in some way, she had offended him.

'Oh, Johann,' she said, her voice soft

and appealing now. 'I didn't mean to bite your head off! I'm upset, too. I feel so terribly guilty, you see. I feel responsible for messing everything up for Jess. I think she really loved him . . . Mike. I hate to think of her being so unhappy — travelling home alone, miserable. And who will take care of Mike?'

'The doctor, the hotel staff. He does not require a nurse for a sprained ankle. He can hobble around with a stick.'

Sally sighed.

'I suppose you are used to such accidents out here, Johann. But he will need someone to talk to, to shop for him.'

Johann pushed aside the cup of chocolate he could not drink. He said quietly, painfully:

'You do not have to find the excuses to me, Sally.'

Once again, the colour rushed into her cheeks. She again looked at him defiantly.

'You haven't actually said so, but you think I'm being a fool, don't you, Johann? Trusting Mike again, I mean.'

tone was meant to be insulting. For a moment she hated Mike. But Johann replied:

'For Sally I do not charge for lessons as she is my friend. For you it will be . . . four hundred schillings.'

'Phew! That's steep!' Now Mike's face was red. Johann had managed very skilfully to make it clear to Mike that he was not, nor likely to become, his friend.

'I'll leave you both to talk it over,' Sally said, slipping down off the bar stool. But Johann at once followed suit.

'I, too, must go. You will excuse us, please?'

'You're not really going, Sally? You've only just come!' Mike protested. 'Even if your friend has to go, you can stay, can't you? Just for five minutes?'

For a brief moment Sally hesitated. She was not strong enough to resist Mike's pleading. She wanted to be with him, to feel the old familiar thrill. Most of all, his extraordinary renewed interest in her was a balm to that terrible aching wound . . . that he could ever have left her. Did he really not understand what his defection had done to her? Had love really meant so little to him that he could cast it off so easily? Or had he gone on loving her all the time?

'I won't think like that — it's weakness!' Sally told herself as she stood hesitating. 'He never did love me . . . I know it, I must never forget it. Anyway, Jess is here and . . . '

'I'm sorry, Mike. Maybe I'll see you tomorrow. Goodnight!'

With a stupendous effort of will she turned away and left the room, Johann beside her. Mike stared after her, his face a mask of bewilderment.

'You have done very well, Sally!' Johann said as they climbed the stairs to the ground floor. 'For one moment I thought you would stay with him. I am glad that you did not.'

Sally gave a deep sigh.

'For one moment *I* thought I'd be weak, too. You've got to help me,

114

Johann. It's quite possible he'll give up trying to see me after tonight, but if he does turn up tomorrow, you'll stay around won't you? No matter what I say, or he says, promise you won't leave me?'

Johann smiled.

'You are a very strange girl, Sally. But I promise. I will be all day the chaperon to you. It is Sunday tomorrow and despite what I say to your Mike, I do not give lessons on a Sunday. If you would like, I can be all day with you. Perhaps as it has not snowed after all, we take the bus to St Anton? I know very nice little place to eat there called Rosanna Stuberl. You like to come?'

'Yes, please!' Sally said with an answering smile. 'After tomorrow, I'll be all right — it's just until he goes.'

'I know!' Now Johann was not smiling. 'I say goodnight now, Sally. Tomorrow I call for you here at ten o'clock. Is all right?'

He gave her the now familiar little bow and disappeared through the front doors. Sally went up in the lift, her body aching with fatigue but her mind wretchedly alert and teeming with thoughts. If only Mike were not here, in Zürs, she could have been happy going around with Johann. They had had a nearly perfect evening at the funny little underground place he had taken her to. Only the knowledge that Mike was so near, within reach, anxious to see her, talk to her, had spoilt everything.

Yet as she undressed, Sally knew she was not being entirely honest with herself. His presence here in Zürs had lent a new desperate excitement to the day. It had revived a lot of terrible, painful memories, yet it had also revived so many perfect ones. She and Mike had been so carefree, so totally happy together. Or nearly always. They had argued at times and there had been the never-ending battle between them because Mike wanted so desperately to make love to her. But most of the while they'd laughed and worked and talked and been happy.

'We have a proverb which perhaps you also know,' said Johann. 'It is 'he who loves once unwisely is to be pitied, but he who loves twice unwisely is a fool!''

Sally drew in her breath sharply. Her eyes were lowered as she replied:

'You've no justification for saying 'unwisely'. It wasn't Mike's fault he couldn't bear the sight of my scars. He felt guilty every time he looked at me. He knew he'd ruined my career, for a while anyway, and there was no positive guarantee I'd ever be able to model again. Even now it is still uncertain. So you see, he tortured himself every time we were together with self-reproaches. I was the one who said I wanted to break up. I could see what it was doing to him.'

'It is easy to talk words!' Johann said quietly, as her voice ceased abruptly. 'It is not always so easy to believe them. If it is truly what you believe, then I cannot say words that will make you think different. It is possible he was not at fault, but it is to me not love that a man can leave his girl when the most she needs him.'

Sally made no reply. One half of her mind accepted only too easily Johann's warning. He was merely telling her what she had told herself many, many times before. But the other half recalled Mike's voice, saying:

'*You begged me to go. I didn't want to leave you. You sent me away!*'

Could she trust him? Was she crazy to believe he did still love her? Obviously Johann thought so, but Johann did not know him. Jess, too, had warned her — and Jess must know him very well.

She felt a shiver of apprehension. She wanted so much to believe the best, and yet everything pointed in the opposite direction. Perhaps Johann was right and she should leave Zürs now — go as far away from Mike as she could; away from temptation — the temptation to believe in his love for her. But there was Bobbie to consider; she most definitely would not wish to leave in the middle of the holiday, quite apart from the terrible waste of money. It was unlikely the hotel would reimburse them for the second week, even if she could persuade Bobbie to go with her. Besides, there was no need to run away. Mike was housebound at his hotel. There was no one to force her to go round there and he could not very easily come here.

But even as she argued with herself, Sally knew that she was deceiving herself. She did not *want* to leave Zürs. She wanted to be with Mike. But for her promise to Johann to attend the tea-dance with him, she would go round there now. Mike would be lonely and longing for company now that Jess had departed.

She looked at her companion with a mixture of affection and exasperation. He had proved such a very good friend; she could not disappoint him over the dance. She really owed him a great deal, for he had somehow succeeded in forcing her out of the inferiority complex with which she'd come on holiday and made her enjoy her stay in a way she'd never have believed possible. It was hard to realise that she had only known Johann for one week. He seemed like a very old and dear friend.

'Johann, what shall I do!' she cried impulsively. 'I'm still in love with him. That's the hell of it!'

'Are you really in love?' Johann replied gently. 'Or are you just in the habit of so thinking? I cannot think that you still have for him the same respect — is this the word?'

Sally gave a hopeless little shrug of her shoulders.

'I don't know. *I don't know!*' she said. 'But I mustn't bore you with my problems. There's no need for you to worry on my behalf. Let's go and dance, shall we?' she added with an effort at cheerfulness that was not lost on him.

For a moment he pondered whether to release her from her promise to go dancing with him. But he pushed the idea from him. If he could only manage in some way to make Sally realise she could be happy without Mike, then all was not yet lost.

As he led her downstairs, he was asking himself just what he hoped to gain by preventing Sally's return to her former fiancé. Was it her happiness he really wanted — or was he being selfish, knowing as he now did that he wanted Sally himself?

They went into the dance room, which was already very crowded, and without waiting to find a table, he drew her into his arms and began to dance. At first, Sally's body was stiff and resistant, but gradually she relaxed and allowed him to hold her nearer to him. Her feet followed his lead effortlessly, and when he met her eyes he saw with a pang of pleasure that she was smiling and happy. United in the movement and music as they had been from their first dance together, they both for a little while forgot Mike and the difficult world outside this one of their own creating.

9

It was gala night at the hotel in St Anton. Bobbie and Basil had joined company with six young student friends of Basil's who each took turns dancing with the only girl in the party. Bobbie, flushed and happy, reckoned she had never had such a wonderful time in England. Seven young men all laughing and arguing as to whose turn it was to dance with her was quite intoxicating. And to add to the excitement, she was very much aware of the watchful eye Basil was keeping on her when she danced with one of his friends. He certainly didn't intend to let any of them usurp his prior right as her escort.

While Bobbie danced, the others sat at the bar drinking iced beer. Their gaiety and high spirits attracted other young people to them, and before long, the choice of drink had become wine.

Several empty and some full bottles were ranged in front of them.

Basil felt particularly happy. He and Bobbie had really hit it off since their first meeting. He found her freckles attractive and her amusing uncomplicated nature equally so. He knew instinctively that this was the kind of girl he could take home and be sure his parents and sisters would approve. Earlier in the evening Bobbie had promised she would make the long trip up north on her next holiday, which she would try to coincide with his. He thought that if her stay at his home was as successful as the holiday here in Zürs, he might even ask her to get engaged. They were both a bit young yet for marriage, and he was by no means sure he, let alone Bobbie, wanted to settle down, but he liked the idea of making her his girl. The fact that all his friends liked her too, made him even more sure of himself.

He tossed down another glass of wine; he knew that he was getting a little tight, but swept the thought to one side. So was everyone else. That was one of the nice things about a ski resort. People seemed to want you to enjoy yourself in an uninhibited way.

He took his turn dancing with Bobbie and twice they bumped into other couples, Bobbie giggling infectiously.

'You've had a glass too many!' she reproved him, but not really seriously. She was having too much fun to mind Basil fooling around a bit. Until now, she had thought him just the tiniest bit over-serious; a bit inclined to be too quiet and thoughtful, although she didn't dislike this serious side to him. All the same, it was nice to know he could be 'daft' occasionally. The more she knew of him, the better she found herself liking him. She had told Sally she meant this little 'romance' to be just for the holiday, but now she wasn't so sure. Basil had asked her to his home and she'd like to go. She liked the sound of his mum and his two sisters and thought it highly complimentary of Basil that he wanted her to meet them. He wouldn't have suggested it if he didn't think they'd approve of her, and obviously he thought a great deal of his family judging by the amount he talked about them.

The evening wore on, not slowly but in a bright, noisy whirl. Some people came in in fancy dress and clowned about on the dance floor for a short while, doing an impromptu cabaret. No one seemed to object. Bobbie, tired now of dancing, sat on the bar stool besides Basil, his arm round her waist, and took occasional sips of wine from his glass.

Just once Bobbie remembered Sally and her good spirits flagged sharply. Poor Sally! It was horrible to think of her worried by that ex-fiancé of hers. It was the greatest shame, in Bobbie's view, that he'd turned up on the scene. Sally was just beginning to relax and enjoy herself with Johann. Bobbie had felt so happy that she'd found a boyfriend and was dancing and ski-ing and having the same good time Bobbie was herself. Now it looked as if Mike Chancery's reappearance was going to ruin everything. But for him, Sally and Johann would be here tonight enjoying the fun. She wondered what Sally was doing at this moment — eleven o'clock. Soon she and Basil would have to start thinking about catching the bus back to Zürs. That is, if they were to catch the bus. Some of the boys had suggested they all share a taxi. She had not seen Sally at dinner as she and Basil had spent the day in St Anton and stayed on to eat at this hotel where it appeared to be Carnival night.

But she could not keep her thoughts concentrated on Sally — or, on anything else for that matter, for long. There was too much to look at, to laugh at, to enjoy. Also she, like Basil, was becoming just a bit tight. She thought she would suggest coffee in a little while to sober them all down a bit, but it seemed a pity to spoil the fun just yet.

She glanced at the band which had been playing practically non-stop all evening. They looked terribly hot. She mentioned it to Basil and the next moment, the boys sent over drinks for the four members of the group.

'Better watch your cash flow!' Bobbie warned, but Basil shrugged his shoulders. 'As long as I've enough for ski-lifts, I'm not worried about tomorrow!' he laughed. 'Tonight is more important, eh?'

A tall fair boy called Tim staggered over to the band to clink glasses with each of them. Then he grabbed the mike and began to sing in a surprisingly good voice. The members of the band seemed quite content to let him continue and he sang three successive songs to the adulation of his friends at the bar and the applause of the room in general.

Encouraged by his success, another boy grabbed Bobbie and gave a demonstration dance to a song which brought an even louder round of applause. When Bobbie, breathless and giggling, was deposited once more at Basil's side, she gasped:

'Go on, Basil. Your turn to perform.'

'Can't!' he replied, draining his glass. ''Bout the only thing I can do is conduct!'

His voice was slurred but the boy, Tim, heard him.

'C'mon!' he cried, slapping Basil on the shoulder. 'The band's packed up for the interval. I'll play and you conduct!'

Egged on by the others, Basil followed Tim onto the now deserted platform. No one seemed to object as they staggered up and Tim sat down at the piano. Basil picked up a drum stick and beat time to the flow of jazz which now came from Tim's able fingers. The rest of their friends, arms linked over each other's shoulders, left the bar to crowd round the platform, laughing and cheering. Basil couldn't see Bobbie among them and none too certainly climbed on to the piano stool, his legs either side of Tim, who was now playing by request 'Let It Be'.

The whole room joined in. Basil forgot Bobbie and made a half-turn with his body so that he could direct the singing. His knee caught Tim's shoulder and as Tim leant forward to give him more room the stool wobbled and tipped backwards. For a few seconds Basil swayed, teetering on the edge of the stool. Then the motion set up a wave of giddiness and the next moment he toppled backwards. There was the most deafening noise as he disappeared, seat first, into the drum kit.

Tim stopped playing. The audience stopped singing. A girl screamed. Basil lay still, his eyes shut, his head swimming. The brittle edges of broken parchment pricked his skin, and made him acutely uncomfortable. But although he wished to move, he seemed to have lost the ability.

Hands reached down and pulled him to his feet. He opened his eyes and met the furious gaze of the drummer. He was shouting at Basil in a rapid flow of German he could not begin to understand. In any event, he was too busy trying to stop his body swaying to be able to concentrate on words. He wished the man would leave him alone.

Tim was motionless. Another member of the band had hold of his arm and was pointing accusingly at the broken drums trying to make Tim understand the seriousness of the situation. Total strangers became involved and the noise was deafening with about twenty people all talking and gesticulating. It was some time before Bobbie was able to push her way through to Basil.

Shouting above the noise the drummer said in English:

'He has finished my drums! Is now no good — finished. Now I have to buy new ones. Your friend is drunk. He must pay.'

White-faced and completely sober, Bobbie stared first at the drums and then at Basil. He grinned sheepishly at her as it dawned on him what he had done.

'What are we going to do?' she asked. 'You'll have to pay him, Basil. Basil, listen for goodness' sake. Can't you understand? We've got to pay for the damage.'

'Ever so sorry!' Basil mumbled. 'Didn't mean to. Fell! Chair tipped me over — plonk, right into the middle of the drums!' He began to laugh, but stopped when Bobbie caught his arm and shook him.

'We've got to find the money,' she said. 'How much have you got, Basil?'

He was still fumbling in his wallet when the hotel manager, fetched by another member of the group, arrived on the scene. Bobbie, Basil, Tim and their friends, together with the band, were asked to go with the manager into the adjoining room. Everyone was rapidly sobering up. The band leader explained in German what had happened. The manager, a short, pasty-faced little man with small mean eyes, regarded the group of English boys with distaste.

'You behave with much disgrace!' he said furiously. 'I do not like such things to happen in my hotel. I will inform the Polizei. You cannot do this kind of thing. You will be severely punished.'

Bobbie pushed forward to the front of the group.

'It was an accident!' she said, equally furiously. 'Basil didn't mean to bust the wretched drums. He fell. It was an accident.'

'So!' said the manager scornfully. 'He fell because he was very much drunk. The Polizei shall deal with this.'

But although he threatened, he made no move towards the telephone at his side. It was only a moment before Bobbie realised this. If he did not mean to call in the police, it must be because he had other ideas. Money? But they had no money — at least, not enough to pay for new drums and bribe the hotel manager to forget the incident.

The man's sharp little eyes were now regarding her unblinkingly. She felt instinctively that she was on the right tack. Somehow, if she were to get Basil out of this mess, they must find some money.

'We will pay for the damage we have done!' she said with as much hauteur as she could muster. 'Every penny — I mean, schilling.'

The manager turned away and began a rapid conversation with the band leader. After a moment, he turned back to Bobbie and said,

'The drummer will have to go to Zürich to replace his instruments. They will cost much money. I, too, require compensation for my band which I have paid for but who cannot now play properly for my guests. We will need at least fourteen thousand schillings.'

'Fourteen thousand schillings!' Bobbie gasped, and Tim, beside her, said:

'That's a bit steep, isn't it? That's about seven hundred pounds for two measly old drums!'

'You prefer I call the Polizei?' the man asked threateningly.

'Tim, no!' Bobbie turned to him and

put a restraining hand on his arm. 'Don't forget we're not in England. We don't know what might happen. They might put Basil in prison — or all of us — we were all in it. And if there's a court case and they claim damages, we might have even more to pay.'

'Yes, but seven hundred quid! Basil moaned. 'I can't put my hands on that kind of money!'

'I could let you have a tenner now!' Tim broke in. 'It was partly my fault. I could raise another fifty when we get back to England.'

'But that's no use!' Bobbie wailed. 'We've got to get the money now.' She turned back to the manager and, concealing her dislike of him, said pleadingly:

'Can you give us a little time to find the money? Obviously we haven't that much on us, but we'll get it, I promise.'

She noticed the band leader and drummer shaking their heads. The manager said bluntly:

'We have no guarantee you will pay

when you go back to England. How do I know you will send the money here to Austria? No, you must pay now or I shall call in the Polizei!'

Bobbie drew a deep breath.

'I'm sure you don't really want the police involved, do you?' she said shrewdly. 'A lot of publicity about people getting drunk in your hotel and being put in prison for it, wouldn't do the tourist trade much good, would it?'

It was a point which had already occurred to him.

'Very well! I give you two days. You can telephone to England. If they can wire the money to you, well and good.'

He turned back to the band leader and obviously instructed them to leave for they filed out, avoiding the eyes of the boys. Bobbie had the feeling they did not like the manager any better than she did, and were sympathetic about the accident once they knew Basil was prepared to pay for new drums. The Austrians were a gentle, friendly people. She did not think they were as mistrusting of the English as the manager appeared to be.

Although she was somehow managing to remain calm outwardly, inwardly she was trembling with apprehension. How on earth was Basil going to find that much money? Would his friends chip in and help? She looked at their faces, sheepish now and no longer very amusing. They had all had far too much too drink. They must have been mad — herself as well, to get so out of control. But it was pointless regretting what was done. The important thing now was to try to put things right.

'May we go back to our hotel now?' she asked the manager. 'We are staying in Zürs, but I will telephone you tomorrow and let you know what steps we are taking to find the money.'

He raised no objection to their departure, but first insisted that they should all write down their names and addresses in England. He had no intention of letting them slip out of his grasp — not that they intended trying to escape the consequences of their actions, Bobbie thought indignantly.

It was now long after midnight and despite the extra cost they no longer felt justified in entertaining, they were forced to take a taxi back to Zürs. During the journey, the boys began to sober up and ways and means of raising money were discussed. The six boys who were Basil's friends all offered to help as much as they could, but even then it still left six hundred pounds outstanding.

Basil groaned. 'I can't telephone home for that much money. I simply haven't got that much saved up. I drew out all my savings to come out here!'

'Perhaps Sally can help us,' Bobbie said, remembering that her friend was the only person she knew who had a large sum of money which she might be prepared to lend Basil. He'd pay it back, of course. He was earning nearly a hundred pounds a week in a factory, he'd told her, and with overtime he could sometimes push his weekly pay packet up even higher. Sally would not have to wait long for the money to be reimbursed.

They dropped the boys at their hotel and paid off the taxi. Then Basil walked up the road to the Edelweiss with Bobbie. The street was deserted. It seemed as if they were the only people in the world.

'I feel awful about all this!' Basil said wretchedly. 'It was such a damn silly thing to do. I'll never get drunk again and that's for sure.'

He sounded so forlorn, Bobbie smiled.

'I expect you will!' she teased gently. 'Try not to worry too much, Basil. I'll talk to Sally first thing in the morning. She's a wonderful person. I know she'll help us if she can.'

'You're the one who is wonderful!' Basil said, stopping to put his arms around her and hug her. 'I couldn't have coped if you hadn't been there. I dare say I'd be in gaol by now. When Mum hears about it, she'll be your slave for life.'

'You're not going to tell her, are you?' Bobbie said, aghast. She knew the reaction there would be from her own parents. They were almost two full generations older than herself, for she'd been born late in their marriage. They seldom saw eye to eye about anything, from music to mini-skirts, to boyfriends. That was why she had left home to join Sally at the flat.

'Oh, Mum'll understand!' Basil said. 'She's like you — a wonderful person. She'll put me in my place, mind you, but she won't go on about it. 'Course I shall tell her.'

Bobbie sighed.

'You're lucky to have a mum like that. I'm looking forward to meeting her.'

Basil looked down at her with a puzzled frown.

'You mean, you'll still plan to come home with me? After this? I'd have thought you'd had enough of me!'

'So I have — at any rate for tonight!' Bobbie laughed. 'Now let's get a move on, Basil, or I'll find myself locked out of my hotel.'

In fact, the hotel door was locked and they had to ring the night bell and arouse the porter, who was none too pleased to be disturbed at three in the morning.

Feeling like a guilty schoolgirl, Bobbie went up in the lift and crept as quietly as she could into hers and Sally's room.

10

When the tea-dance ended, Johann took Sally back to the lounge for a drink before she went upstairs to change for dinner. He was on the point of inviting her to meet him after the meal when the receptionist came over and handed Sally a note. It was from Mike, saying he was in great pain, had had to call in the doctor again, and would be grateful if she could go round at once. Wordlessly, she handed the note to Johann.

'I'm sorry,' she said when he handed it back to her without remark. 'I'll have to go.'

He put down his glass and met Sally's apologetic glance, his own eyes filled with bitterness.

'I suppose for these last hours I have known that you preferred to be with him. It is your life, Sally, and so it is for you to arrange as the best you think.'

'Please try to understand!' she said, but he had turned away to pay for their drinks and was already on his feet, bowing as he bent to kiss her hand lightly in farewell.

'Perhaps I see you at the lesson tomorrow,' he said, his voice stiff. 'I look for you. Good night, Sally!'

She stared after him, her eyes uneasy as she watched him walk away. It was almost as if she were watching a friend walk out of her life. She wanted his approval, his understanding, but knew she was being unreasonable to expect either. It was natural he should think badly of Mike. Johann didn't know him as she did. And besides, she suddenly realised, he was probably a little jealous. It was even possible Johann was half-way to falling in love with her, and he could hardly be expected to welcome a rival on the scene.

But Sally could not waste any more time thinking about Johann. She must hurry round to Mike . . . he needed her.

The mere thought was exhilarating, exciting.

Mike was having his dinner on a tray in bed when she arrived a quarter of an hour later at his hotel. He pushed the tray to one side and held out his arms.

'Sally, darling! I thought you'd never come,' he greeted her. 'If you knew how long the hours have been lying here, waiting. I wasn't even sure you would come. You didn't ring me back. Your hotel receptionist said you were out when I rang.' His voice was slightly accusing. Sally blushed.

'I was at the tea-dance with Johann!' she admitted truthfully. She saw Mike's dark brows draw together in a frown. 'I didn't get your message until the dance finished. I came at once!'

His expression changed and he beckoned her to come nearer. She walked across to him slowly, almost hesitantly. Mike lifted the tray on to the bedside table and drew Sally down beside him, keeping her hands imprisoned as he leant forward to kiss her.

But she drew away, her thoughts and emotions in confusion.

'Your message said you'd had to have the doctor again, Mike. Is the pain very bad? Are you all right? Has . . . has Jess really gone?'

Mike released her hands and lit a cigarette, eyeing Sally's profile speculatively.

'Yes, she's gone. In a way, I'm glad. It was all over between us ages ago, Sally. Not that there ever was much. I was fond of her, but . . . well, I don't want to be disloyal, but she took everything far too seriously. I think she half hoped I'd fall in love with her despite the fact that she knew I was still in love with you. I wanted a simple working arrangement and she wanted a more personal one.'

Sally discovered she had been holding her breath while she listened to his explanation. She had not really thought it out, but now she knew she had had a horribly guilty feeling all along about Jess. She had somewhere deep down inside herself hated the thought that she was hurting the other girl — as she herself had once been hurt. Now that Mike had explained how it was between them, she could feel free to think only of herself.

'Look at me, Sally!' Mike was commanding in that well-remembered forceful tone. 'Don't you trust me? Don't you believe I love you? What's wrong between us?'

Now she did turn and look at him fully, her eyes wide and questioning.

'I want to trust you, Mike — to believe you. You say you always loved me, yet you never tried to get in touch with me once I came out of hospital. You never wrote . . . phoned . . . '

'But, my darling, you asked me not to. Had you forgotten? You told me to forget you — to give you a chance to forget me. That was the way *you* wanted it. Don't you think I suffered dreadfully all those months? Don't you realise what a torture they were for me, knowing you were better? Don't you think I was waiting all the time for *you* to get in touch with *me?*'

'Oh, Mike!' Sally whispered. 'If I could believe that . . . '

'How can you doubt it?' he broke in, drawing her back into his arms. 'I've never loved anyone but you, Sally. Finding you here accidentally like this has been like a miracle. I can still hardly believe it. Tell me you do still love me. You do, don't you, Sally? You haven't found anyone else? That Austrian guy? He doesn't mean anything to you, does he?'

With Mike's arms round her, his lips almost touching hers, she could scarcely remember Johann's existence. This was a total return to the past — to the remembered happiness of days before her accident; to dreams and hopes and prayers. This was Mike, wanting her, loving her, needing her — just as it used to be in the old days.

His arms tightened round her and she felt her heart pounding so fiercely she could not breathe. Once again, a knock on the door separated them, breaking the spell of the moment. It was the floor waiter, bringing Mike's coffee and brandy he had ordered and to collect his tray.

Sally had had no dinner, and Mike, on hearing this, insisted upon ordering a meal to be sent up for her. She could eat very little of it when it came, but enough at least to satisfy Mike. To please him, she drank some wine, but refused the brandy he wanted her to have. In the end he drank it for her. His face, pale when she had arrived, was now flushed. Sally looked at him anxiously.

'Ought you to drink, Mike, if you're having drugs?' she asked. Mike looked annoyed.

'Now don't start mothering me!' he said. 'I'm only taking pain killers. As a matter of fact, I wish I hadn't taken them now. They're making me so damn sleepy, I want to be on my best form with you, Sally — not half doped!'

But despite his wishes, the day had taken its toll of him. With two double brandies on top of the painkillers, it was all he could do to keep his eyes open.

'I think you should sleep,' Sally said, seeing how drowsy he had become. She shook out his pillows and he lay back on them, his eyes closing.

'Don't leave me!' he begged her.

Sally smiled.

'I'll come back tomorrow. I can spend all day with you,' she promised. 'It's nearly ten o'clock now, anyway, so I ought to be going. I'll come round first thing after breakfast, Mike.'

He tried to cling to her hand but his fingers had no strength and in a moment or two he was fast asleep. Tenderly, Sally smoothed the hair back from his forehead and stood looking down at him. Asleep, he looked so much younger, so defenceless. It was impossible to think of that other Mike, restless, evasive, cruel in his desire to be gone, to desert her when she had needed him so desperately. Maybe it had been her own stupid fault and she had only imagined that Mike wanted his freedom; that the sight of her revolted him. Maybe because she had feared it, she had passed the thought to him and that had she said nothing, done nothing, he would never have left her.

It was what she wanted to believe, to think, and looking at him now it was easy enough to believe. He had always loved her. She was the one who had brought about their split up — not Mike.

She bent and kissed him. He did not stir. She drew back the curtains, opened the windows and turned off the lights. Then she removed the tray from the room so that the waiter, calling for it, would not disturb him. With one last look at his sleeping form, she closed the door and went down in the lift, her eyes thoughtful, her heart strangely at peace. It was useless, she thought, to try to fight against Fate. If Fate intended them to be together again, it would work out that way. Already it seemed as if some powerful force were doing its best to bring them together again. Even Mike's accident this morning seemed like a stroke of luck that was intended to keep them near to each other.

Sally walked home through the cold night air, breathing deeply, watching her breath rise like steam in the sub-zero temperature. She wondered briefly where Bobbie was; if Johann would be very upset when she did not appear for her ski lesson tomorrow. But her thoughts would not stay away from Mike for long. Now that the pain of the past was wearing away beneath Mike's repeated assurances that he had never stopped loving her, she could contemplate a stage beyond sheer surprise and joy at this reunion with him. She could allow herself the luxury of remembering days before the accident when she and Mike had been so happy together.

Of course, she told herself as she reached her hotel and went up to her bedroom, there had been unhappy days, too. The times they had quarrelled and she had doubted whether they were really so well suited. But Mike had a quicksilver artistic temperament and she had known even then that she must make many adjustments, many allowances for him. It wouldn't be a marriage of equality — she'd realised that. Mike had to be the leader, the dominant partner, but she had been content to accept this and to bask in his shadow. Most of their rows, brief, stormy, violent, had been caused by Mike's jealousy of her success as a model. He had not liked the limelight deflected from his orbit. But that, too, she had understood, for his career was everything to him and hers of very minor importance to her. He was the one thing in the world that really mattered to her — not her job. But she was old-fashioned enough to believe that a man's career was of prime importance and she had not sought fame for herself as she had desired it for Mike. What had hurt was that he should, at times, blame her for the adulation she received when she had only wanted success for him.

Sally stood at her window, staring out into the starlit darkness. The past seemed suddenly very close. It was all too easy to recall how those rows had ended — with a reconciliation that was as violent as the quarrel itself. It was almost as if they had continued to fight each other — Mike to prove a purely physical domination and Sally desperately clinging to what little self-control she had not to give in. It was not that she was afraid of sex . . . only of the half-awakened desires in herself which she knew instinctively would become ungovernable once she gave herself fully to the man she loved. Her surrender, when it came, would be total — complete, and there would be no turning back. She had known it and, for some not altogether understood reason, had feared to reach that point in her relationship with Mike. It was almost, looking back, as if she had had a presentiment of what was to come. Bad as those long, long months had been, it would, she was sure, have been a hundred times worse if she and Mike had ever been lovers.

Slowly Sally undressed, bathed and climbed into bed. Lying there, warm and relaxed, it was all too easy to give way to the luxury of dreaming about marriage to Mike. They had been drawn to each other from the first moment of meeting. It had been a case of instant mutual attraction. Strangely enough, she hadn't really liked him as a person. She'd thought him self-opinionated and domineering and even a little affected. But in the end, his attraction had proved too strong for her to refuse the persistent telephone calls, the requests for dates, and she had agreed to go out with him. From then on she was lost, no longer able to see his personality separate from the man. It had always been predominantly a sexual attraction although, as was inevitable, she had grown to see only the likable facets of his nature and to make allowances for the traits she had at first disliked.

As she grew drowsy, Sally's thoughts reverted to her companion of the last week. How different was her friendship with Johann. Here she had grown to know and like the person he was, and only much later discover that he, too, could attract her. It was silly to pretend that she had not enjoyed being kissed by him; being held so tightly in his arms as they danced in perfect unison. But for Mike, she might easily have lost her head — and her heart — to Johann. He was sweet — an adjective he might not care to hear used about himself but which described him so well. Even Bobbie had said so! He was kind, too, and as far as she could judge, totally unselfish. She hoped very much he would not be too hurt by her desertion of him in favour of Mike; for it would have to come to that. She would want to spend every free moment now with Mike. Somehow she must make Johann understand that it was not through any failing on his part — merely that she had never stopped being Mike's girl . . .

Sally fell into a deep sleep from which only with the greatest difficulty could Bobbie arouse her when she came in in the early hours of the morning.

'Sally, do wake up, please!' Bobbie pleaded. 'It's terribly important. Something ghastly has happened!'

Sally opened her eyes and tried to concentrate on Bobbie's words. Her friend's white anxious face finally roused her from her drowsy state and she sat up, brushing the fair hair away from her face.

'What is it? What's wrong?' she asked.

To her consternation, Bobbie burst into tears. Only by degrees could Sally make sense of the garbled account of the fateful evening in St Anton.

'I don't know what we're going to do!' Bobbie ended with a gulp. 'I'm so worried, Sal. Do you think you *could* help us?'

'You know I will if I can!' Sally said promptly. But her voice was not very hopeful. 'I just wish I thought the bank would send some money. Six hundred pounds! I could probably raise fifty if we economised like mad for the last week out here, but six hundred . . . '

'I know!' Bobbie wailed. 'In a way it's Basil's worry rather than mine, but I promised to try and help and it *was* partly my fault. I didn't have so much to drink as all the others and I could see things were getting out of hand. I ought to have stopped them.'

Sally put a hand comfortingly on Bobbie's arm.

'No good crying over spilt milk. Anyway, it's late and you need sleep. We can't do anything tonight so get to bed, Bobbie, and we'll sort it out somehow tomorrow.'

Whilst a tired, dispirited Bobbie made preparations for the night, Sally lay back on her pillow and tried to find a solution. She could have asked Aunt

Margaret to have some money transferred from England but she was away in Scotland with a friend and Sally had no idea where to contact her. She herself had drawn all but a few pounds from her current account to pay for the holiday and since the rest of her money was invested, she doubted she could arrange a loan at this distance, and Bobbie had said the cash was needed immediately. She had plenty of it, if only she knew how to get hold of it! Strange to think she was rich! Not that a fortune would ever compensate for the accident and what it had done to her.

Suddenly, Sally sat upright, frowning. Memories of the accident had brought back the thought of Mike. Perhaps he could help. She knew he must have some Austrian money. In all probability, as it was a business trip, Mike had been financing it. He might have travellers cheques.

When Bobbie came out of the bathroom, Sally was smiling happily.

'I think we can stop worrying,' she told her friend. 'Mike will lend the money. I'll go round first thing tomorrow and explain what has happened.'

Bobbie drew a long sigh of relief.

'You're wonderful, Sal!' she cried happily. 'I never thought of *him*. But, Sal, do you really think he'll want to part with his money for *me?* After all, he hardly knows me. It isn't as if it is you who wants it. I'm almost a stranger to him.'

'You're my friend,' Sally replied simply. 'I know he'll help if he can.'

But Sally was wrong. Mike was far from eager to help.

'I've only got about three hundred pounds and a few travellers cheques!' he told her. 'By the time I've paid the hotel bill and my doctor's bill, there'd be nothing left if I bail out your friend. It virtually means I'd have to go back to England at once.'

Sally sat on the edge of Mike's bed, her hopes falling.

'I thought you were going home anyway, Mike. You said you were only here for the weekend.'

Mike reached over and caught her hand, squeezing it softly.

'That's before I knew you were here, darling. You don't really think I mean to go home a day sooner than I have to — not now.'

Sally sighed. She could understand Mike's point of view. She didn't want him to go either. The thought of staying on in Zürs without him held little appeal. If he went home, she would want to go, too. But she was committed to staying. It was very unlikely that in the middle of their holiday the hotel would release her and Bobbie from their booking. But Mike hadn't booked. He'd managed to get a cancelled room. He admitted now that he had not committed himself to remaining longer than the weekend, although the hotel had told him yesterday he could retain the room for a further week if he required it.

'Look, Sal, you can't honestly expect me to pack up and go home just because some of your juvenile friends have landed themselves in a mess. It isn't any concern of mine — or yours. Let them work out their own problems. Besides, I couldn't possibly travel with this leg. I had a hell of a night.'

Although Sally was instantly sympathetic, a tiny part of her mind registered the selfishness of Mike's reasoning. He was thinking only of himself. True though it was that neither Bobbie nor Basil were his friends, she had asked Mike to help her, Sally, to help them.

'I don't see what they can do!' she said unhappily. 'It would be too awful if the hotel manager in St Anton called in the police. I *have* to find a way to help them, Mike. I promised Bobbie.'

'Forget it and come here and kiss me!' Mike said, grinning at her disarmingly. 'Do you realise you've been in this room nearly ten minutes and you haven't kissed me yet?'

He tried to pull her closer, but Sally

felt herself stiffening.

'Mike, I can't forget about it,' she said. 'I'm sorry if I can't talk or think about anything else but it's been on my mind all night.'

'*You've* been on *my* mind!' Mike said in a low, meaningful voice. 'I'm madly in love with you, Sally. You realise that, don't you? I can't bear you out of my sight now. You look beautiful, darling — good enough to eat! Please come here and kiss me.'

She half inclined towards him, weakening as always to that gentle persuasive tone. But Bobbie's white, anxious face came to the front of her mind. She was waiting for Sally at the hotel. 'Hurry back as quickly as you can, Sal!' she'd begged. 'I'll be on tenterhooks until I know it's going to be all right.' And Sally had promised not to be more than half an hour at the most.

'Mike, I have to get this trouble sorted out before — before anything else!' she faltered. 'Please try to understand. Bobbie's in a dreadful state and I promised to help. She is my friend even if she isn't yours, and she's been a truly wonderful friend to me. I can't think of myself now. Can't you see that?'

The gentle smile on Mike's face gave way to a downward twist of his mouth.

'The trouble with you is you're too soft, Sally. You always were. We can't all be as noble as you!'

Sally caught her lower lip between her teeth. Mike's criticism hurt her dreadfully. She wasn't trying to be noble — just to help a friend. Mike made it sound as if she were a boring do-gooder.

'Oh, for pity's sake, Sally, don't look so hurt!' Mike's voice was soft again. 'I didn't mean to be nasty to you, darling. It's just that I'm a little jealous. I've been waiting all night for this morning to come so that I could enjoy your company, and all you can talk about is this tiresome mess your friends have got themselves into. Can't you give me a few minutes of your time?'

Sally smiled a little shakily.

'I want to, Mike, but perhaps I've got a one-track mind. I can't seem to think about anything else. We have to find that six hundred pounds this morning. I can't sit here talking to you when time's short. You must see that.'

Mike lay back against his pillow and drew a big sigh.

'Okay, so I come second. Well, I suppose I should expect that. You don't still love me in the same way, do you, Sally? Or else you want to get your own back on me because you think I once hurt you.'

'Oh, Mike!' Sally protested, her face flushed and her eyes angry. 'That isn't fair! I'm not trying to hurt you. You just don't want to understand. It's you who doesn't love me. If you did, you'd want to help me.'

'Damn it, of course I'd help you if I could!' Mike cried. 'But you don't honestly expect me to pack up my bags and go home just to get that idiotic boy Basil out of a mess, do you? Why should I?'

'No reason!' Sally said almost inaudibly.

For a moment neither spoke. Mike looked at the girl's face partly with irritation and partly with desire. She was very beautiful. He no longer noticed the scar. Her skin was a perfect shade of golden brown and her green eyes looked enormous, and even more attractive when they flashed at him with such feeling. He wanted to see them go deep and soft and full of love the way he remembered. He wanted to make love to her — yet it was all too obvious that she wasn't in the least concerned about *him* this morning.

'Look, Sally, why not ask that Austrian boyfriend of yours to help. No doubt he has Austrian money and to spare. Anyone can see he's crazy about you.' Mike warmed to his own idea. 'That's solved all your problems. Get a loan from him and pay the wretched bill and come back to me as quickly as you can. What about it, darling? A brilliant solution, I think, even if I did evolve it myself.'

Sally let out her breath. Her mind seemed to be whirling with mixed emotions. Johann *would* have Austrian money, but she couldn't ask him to lend her so big an amount as that. He was a stranger — or if not a stranger exactly, too new a friend to borrow money from. And surely Mike of all people must realise she couldn't put herself under an obligation to Johann — just because he *was* fond of her. 'Crazy about you!' Those were the words Mike had used. They confused her. She hadn't really thought of Johann feeling that way about her. *Was* it true? Or was Mike just saying it without having thought much about it? Could Johann have fallen in love with her and she herself not realised it?

'Well, what's the problem now?' Mike interrupted her thoughts. 'I'm sure he won't refuse to lend it.'

'But, Mike ... ' She broke off, unable to put into words her reluctance to take advantage of Johann's fondness for her.

'Well?' Mike prompted.

'I can't ask him to lend me money.'

Mike shrugged his shoulders.

'No, I can't ask him!' Sally burst out. 'I just *can't!* Not Johann.'

'What's so special about Johann?' Mike said pointedly. 'What have you got to be afraid of, Sally? Think he might try to take advantage of you once you're under an obligation?'

Sally's cheeks were once again suffused with colour.

'He'd never do that! You don't know him, Mike, or you wouldn't suggest such a thing. It's a horrible thing to say about anyone.'

Mike's eyebrows were raised, his eyes angry and jealous.

'You seem to have a very fine opinion of him. I'm beginning to wonder just what has been going on between you two.'

Sally jumped to her feet and stood staring down at Mike, her eyes perplexed and angry.

'You're being pathetic, Mike, and I'm not staying to hear any more. But since you've asked, there's been absolutely nothing between us. I've kissed him once and that's all. We're friends — nothing more.'

Mike's face softened. He held out both hands.

'Now come on, Sally. Don't get on your high horse, darling. I was only teasing. You can't blame me for being a little jealous, can you? It's a compliment if you stop to think about it. It's only because I love you I can't bear to think of you caring for anyone else. Come here and kiss me, sweetheart. Then I'll let you go.'

Sally hesitated. In a way she could understand him being jealous but for a moment she had found herself hating and despising him for his remarks about Johann. They had somehow sullied what had been a perfectly innocent and valued relationship. It was almost as if he, Mike, had succeeded in reducing it to a lower level where friendship in its pure, true sense had never existed. If Mike had bothered to ask her about Johann, she could have told him that there was no reason at all for him to be jealous. He'd jumped to the wrong conclusion.

'Darling, do come here. It's so unfair to stay out of reach when you know my leg won't let me jump out of bed and come to you!'

She relaxed and let herself go to him. A moment later she was in his arms and he was kissing her violently. She felt his mouth hard and demanding upon her own, and for an instant she responded, returning his kiss with equal ardour. But then the village church bell tolled out the hour, bringing her back to a sense of time and urgency and she drew away.

'I have to go back to Bobbie!' she protested breathlessly. 'Let me go, Mike, *please*. I'll come back — when it's all sorted out. But let me go now, *please*, Mike.'

He tried again to kiss her but this time she did not respond and with a sigh he released her.

'I suppose I'll have to let you go,' he said, reaching for a packet of cigarettes and lighting one. 'You know, you've changed, Sally. You're much harder than you used to be — more independent. I suppose that's only to be expected. But there was a time when ... when nothing would have made you leave me when you knew how much I wanted you.'

'Oh, Mike, don't!' Sally said, straightening her hair and moving away from the bed to put as much space between them as possible. 'You know I don't want to go. I just have to. Please try to understand.'

He shrugged, unsmiling, and Sally had to leave him knowing that he was disappointed in her. She had always wanted his approval; had never been happy when she knew she had somehow upset or displeased him. Now that old feeling of inadequacy was back with all-too-well-remembered poignancy.

It wasn't until she was outside the hotel walking back along the icy road to the Edelweiss that she realised he had proved himself inadequate, too — not as a lover but as a friend. He wasn't going to help Bobbie and Basil. He didn't intend to lend them the money — not the six hundred pounds or even a part of it. He hadn't even offered to lend them a few pounds. 'Ask Johann!' he had suggested.

But it was the last thing she wanted or *could* bring herself to do.

11

As Sally entered the hotel foyer, Bobbie came rushing to meet her, her face as bright as Sally's was downcast.

'Sal, it's all right. Everything's worked out!'

'You mean you haven't got to pay the fine?' Sally asked as she removed her anorak and gloves and hung them in the hall.

'No, not that. We've still got to pay up, but Johann is going to lend us the money. Isn't it wonderful of him? I'm so relieved, Sal — you just can't imagine.'

'Johann!' Sally echoed. 'Oh, Bobbie, you haven't asked *him*, have you? I . . .'

'No, silly!' Bobbie broke in, her freckled face beaming. 'He came round to find you and when I told him you'd gone to see Mike, he stayed on to have coffee with me. Then he asked me why I was so gloomy and I told him and explained that you'd gone to Mike to ask him to help. That's when he offered of his own accord to lend me the money. He said we should have gone to him in the first place. He's in the lounge now . . . over by the window.'

She broke off, realising that there was no answering smile in Sally's eyes.

'What's wrong, Sal?' she asked anxiously. 'Have I made things awkward somehow? Has Mike lent the money, too? If so, I've only to tell Johann I don't need it after all.'

'No, Mike can't lend the money. He hasn't enough to spare.' Sally forced the words through her unwilling lips. Bobbie shrugged.

'Well, quite frankly, Sal, I didn't think he would. After all, I'm not a friend of his, am I? Why should he put himself out for me — or Basil.'

'Why should Johann?' Sally asked involuntarily.

Bobbie gave a puzzled little frown.

'Well, come to think of it, I really don't know. It just didn't strike me as odd that he should. Of course, I know he's your friend, but somehow I think he'd have helped me out even if he didn't know you. He's such a *kind* person, isn't he?'

Sally nodded. She was not quite sure why, but she felt utterly miserable. She ought to be happy for Bobbie that her worries were over, and yet her own mood was one of confusion and discomfort. She knew it had something to do with the comparison between the two men's reactions. Mike had been concerned only with himself. Yet it wasn't altogether fair to make those comparisons.

She had no time for deeper reflections as Bobbie was already guiding her to the table where Johann was sitting. He rose at once to his feet and kissed her hand.

'You will have coffee, Sally?' he asked.

She tried to return his smile but

could only nod. If he sensed her embarrassment he did not refer to it, but ordered the coffee and began to talk quite normally about the ski-ing conditions. The lifts had been stopped for the morning, as it was so icy, ski-ing would have been dangerous. Hence the reason for his unexpected freedom during the morning.

When the waitress brought Sally's coffee, Bobbie stood up and excused herself saying she must go round to see Basil and tell him the good news. She shook Johann's hand warmly and thanked him again in her exuberant way for his offer to help. Johann smiled back at her.

'It is my pleasure!' he said. 'I will go with your Basil later to the bank and draw what money he requires. Please to tell him I am at his disposal.'

When Bobbie had gone, Sally turned to Johann.

'It is more than kind of you, Johann,' she said. 'But I'm not at all happy about it. We've no right to impose on you in this way.'

'Impose?' Johann echoed, his grey-blue eyes gently teasing. 'This is English word I do not know of the meaning.'

Suddenly, Sally found herself smiling, too.

'I'm sure you understand the meaning very well, Johann. It just isn't right that you should be involved in Bobbie's troubles. They aren't even Bobbie's troubles, really, except that she was in the party that caused the damage.'

'This I know!' Johann said, nodding. 'She have told all about it. It is pity you and I did not go, too, to keep them on good behaviour, no?'

'I wish we had!' Sally said fervently. 'But seriously, Johann, have you thought about this loan? It may be weeks before we can repay you. Of course, the moment I get home, I'll go to my bank and see if anything can be done. But it's sure to take time.'

'It is not important!' her companion replied. 'I have savings from which this will come. I do not need back the money quickly.'

'You make it all seem so simple!' Sally sighed. 'I'd feel so much happier if I thought there was a quicker way of repaying you.'

'You are please not to worry, Sally. It is to stop you worrying that I have offered to lend Bobbie the money. I do not wish your holiday here in Zürs spoilt by such things.'

Despite herself, Sally blushed. Deep down she had known that it was for her Johann had made the gesture.

'You are very kind,' she said softly.

Suddenly, Johann took possession of her hand. He held it tightly between his own.

'I want that we should be friends, Sally. I think it has made very much difference to me knowing you. I would like that we should always be friends. Perhaps I come to England, yes? To visit you?'

'Oh, Johann, yes! That would be wonderful. You could stay with us — with my aunt, I mean — that is, if you'd like to. You'd like my Aunt Margaret, and I know she would like you. Will you really come and be our guest, Johann?'

'Of course, now you have invited me. It will be excellent for my English and perhaps also I can arrange myself work for the summer in your country.'

He still held her hand and Sally became conscious of it. Almost as if sensing her feelings, Johann released it.

'That we should be good friends it is necessary we should be honest together, Sally. Do you agree?'

Without waiting for her assent, he continued:

'I think it is right you should know that I have the great affection for you. I know, also, that you do not feel as I do. I think you have still the love for Mike, no? Therefore, I do not have the hope to be more to you than friend. I wish you to know that this for me is very big thing.'

Sally was speechless. The last thing she had expected was a declaration of this kind from Johann — at this moment, and in so calm and matter-of-fact a tone. She did not know how to answer him.

'Please do not let what I have told to you spoil this friendship,' he went on calmly. 'I have thought much about my feelings for you. I have told to myself it is perhaps best that I do not see you no more. Now I am decided this is not good. I want we should be friends. For your sake, I try also to know and to like Mike. I will seek to be good friends to him also. I hope also he will like me.'

Sally felt a rush of hot tears prick her eyelids. She blinked them back and hurriedly lit a cigarette.

'I don't see how Mike or anyone else could help liking you, Johann. I think you are one of the nicest people I know. I am very flattered that you should ... that you should feel as you do about me. I can and do return your friendship — if that is enough?'

Johann's face was turned slightly away from her now so that she could not see the sadness in his eyes.

'Once I thought never to love another girl after I lost my Lisa. Now I have changed the mind. Perhaps when I am come to England, I will meet other English girl such as you, Sally. Maybe I find one to marry, no?'

'I hope so!' Sally cried softly. 'I do hope so, Johann. You'd make some girl so happy. I wish . . . '

She broke off, suddenly aware that she had been about to say she wished there had never been a Mike; that she could have fallen in love with Johann. But of course, it wasn't true.

'And you will find happiness again with Mike?' Johann's voice broke in on her thoughts.

'I think so!' Sally said, sighing. 'I think he really does love me, Johann. Only he's a different kind of person from you. He's not quiet and gentle and thoughtful the way you are. It's because of his artistic temperament — up one minute and down the next. He's so violent in his emotions. I suppose he isn't a very restful sort of person to love, but . . . well, one can't choose the place where one's heart goes. I've always loved him — since I left school. I can't imagine not caring about him. I tried so hard to hate him . . . but I couldn't. All I did was bury my feelings below the surface. I know he has faults — perhaps more than most people. But I still love him.'

'He is lucky man, Sally. I do not think many girls forgive as you have done.'

'Forgive?' Sally repeated. 'Oh, you mean about our breaking up. But it was really my fault, Johann. Mike truly believed that was what I wanted. I told him so, and I succeeded in convincing him. I can't blame him for it now I know he never stopped loving me.'

'And Jess?' Johann's voice was so quiet Sally had to strain to catch his words.

'Jess? Mike was not in love with her. I think she loved him, but she meant no more to him than . . . than his model. I know Mike. He has to feel involved with the model he's working with. Perhaps he was fond of her but he didn't love her. He told me so.'

Johann remained silent. It was not for him to point out to Sally that she might not be wise to take Mike's word for anything. After all, he did not know the man — except through Sally's eyes . . . and with a brief glimpse through Jess's eyes. It was natural that he should feel antipathetic to the man who held Sally's heart. Jealousy would bias him against Mike even if his own instinct was not already against him.

He had no doubt in his own mind that he loved Sally . . . so much that he could not bring himself to stop seeing her although the sensible side of his nature warned him the easiest way was a quick clean break. But he didn't want to make that break. He wanted to keep in touch with her. His motives were not entirely sentimental. It had crossed his mind that if Mike could let Sally down once, it could happen a second time.

He would not want such a thing to happen with his knowledge. But for Mike, he might have had a chance to win Sally's affection if not her love.

Johann's nature was a generous one. He would have lent Bobbie the money she needed regardless of his feelings for Sally. He had always been ready to help people in trouble and he knew he could trust the girl. She might be irresponsible but not dishonest, and it was his policy to trust until he discovered his trust was misplaced. But he was glad to have been given this chance to help the girl, and through her, Sally. It would mean he had a reason to keep in touch with her, and if she had really meant her invitation to him to visit her and her aunt in England, he had every intention of taking it up. His plans for the summer were unmade. There was nothing to prevent his going to England if he wished. He had worked very hard for many years and had earned a holiday.

'Tell me about England!' he said to Sally, wishing to get off the subject of Mike. It hurt him too much to listen to her talk of the man she loved, although he knew he would have to get used to it if he was to continue seeing her. He would have to accept her engagement, and ultimately her marriage, but he hoped the latter would be some time off.

He listened while Sally talked, not really taking in the meaning of her words so much as enjoying the soft gentle voice filled with enthusiasm for her country. He found great happiness when she spoke of simple things they would enjoy together — she and him.

'We'll hire a little car, Johann, and drive up to the Lake District. You'll love the hills — not a bit like your mountains but just as beautiful in their own way. Can you drive? I expect Aunt Margaret would come with us as she loves the Lakes. And we'll 'do' London, of course. I'll guide you round the Tower and you can take photographs of

Buckingham Palace!'

There was no mention of Mike. Johann noticed the omission and wondered why. Would such charming expeditions bore him? Or did Sally feel it would be more polite to leave him out? It puzzled him, but he was content to leave Mike out of the conversation. If these plans ever came to fruition, he'd be glad to leave him out of the expeditions, too!

'It'll be such fun!' Sally cried, her cheeks warm with excitement. 'There are so many things I want to do, too, but I've never had the time or the money. Now, because of the money from my accident, I can travel the way I always wanted. You wouldn't mind Aunt Margaret coming, too? She's been so wonderful to me and I know she'd enjoy it all as much as we would. If anyone deserves a break, she does.'

'Tell me about her!' Johann said. But laughing, Sally refused.

'No, I'd rather you met her and

found out all about her for yourself. I just know you'll like each other. It's going to be wonderful. I almost wish it was summer now.'

It was all Johann could do not to bend over and kiss her eager, excited face. His heart was twisting with a mixture of pleasure and pain. If it were not for Mike, how perfect it would be sitting here making plans with Sally for their next holiday . . . together. How happy he would be to think that the aunt she was so fond of should like and approve of him! How ecstatic the thought of Sally so radiant because she loved him, Johann . . .

But he trod quickly on such reflections. If he was to derive any happiness at all from their friendship, he must not think of love. To do so, or even to remind her how he felt about her, was to jeopardise everything. He must never let her know what he suffered even as he enjoyed the pleasure of her company.

'You will not be working in the

summer?' he asked.

Sally grimaced.

'I suppose I'll have to do some work, but I think I shall leave my secretarial job. I've never really enjoyed it. I'd like to get back to modelling but that depends on Mike and on this . . . ' She touched the scar on her face.

'It is now not hardly to be noticed,' Johann told her. 'I think you make very beautiful pictures, Sally. It is difficult for me when I look at you to remember you are the same girl I saw in the bus only so few days ago. Then you have the head so, bent down very low, and the eyes are not smiling, and you are white like the ghost.'

Sally laughed.

'If I have changed it's entirely due to you, Johann. You have been marvellous. You restored all my self-confidence. I don't *feel* the same person. Looking back, I think I'd developed a sort of complex about my face. I always imagined everyone was staring at me. I suppose I actually attracted their attention because of the way I kept my face hidden as much as possible. Now I behave normally people don't seem to notice I'm not normal.'

'But you are normal, Sally, except that you are so much prettier than most girls. It is for this people stare. I understand why it is you make the good model . . . you have the face one wishes to look at not once but twice and again.'

'Mike and I haven't discussed it,' Sally said shyly, 'but I *hope* he'll think as you do. I'll talk to him about it this afternoon when I go back to see him after lunch. Please, Johann, will you lunch here at the hotel with Bobbie and me? We'd like you to be our guest. Will you?'

There was no need for Sally to plead with him so persuasively. He was only too willing to stay; to spend as many precious minutes as were left to him with her. He felt that time was running out all too fast. A few more days and she would be going back to England,

and it would be months before he saw her again. Even the hours of the few remaining days would be sorely limited now Mike was here. He could not expect her to go dancing with him in the evenings. Perhaps even her ski-ing lessons would be discontinued. The thought dismayed him.

'Would you permit me once before you go home to take you dancing again?' he asked abruptly. 'If you were to ask permission from your Mike, then he would not be angry if you came out with me. I love so much to dance with you and will not again have the chance.'

'Of course I will!' Sally cried. 'I'd like it, too. I'm sure Mike won't mind.'

But even as she spoke the words, she was not so sure. Mike was already jealous of Johann. He would be unlikely to welcome the idea of her going out alone with him. On the other hand, he had suggested she put herself under an obligation to Johann by borrowing money from him. He could hardly complain if she felt she owed it to Johann to give him a little of her time and company.

All the same, Sally told herself ruefully, it would perhaps be as well not to mention to Mike that Johann had actually professed himself to be a little in love with her. She wanted to stay friends with Johann, and if she were really going to see a lot of him during his visit to England that summer, it was easier for them all if Mike liked and approved of Johann; or at the very least accepted him.

Sally tried to push from her mind the memory of Mike's possessiveness in earlier days. He had taken strange unwarranted dislikes to so many of her friends; made her stop seeing them. He had even wanted her to break with Aunt Margaret, although she had never once considered doing so. Despite her love for her aunt, Mike had not hesitated to try to belittle her, run her down, put the blame on Aunt Margaret for the rift between her and himself. Perhaps he had not been altogether unjustified. Aunt Margaret hadn't liked him though she had tried hard in the early days to conceal it. But she was never warm and giving to him the way she usually was to all Sally's friends.

At least, Sally thought, there was little doubt that her aunt would love Johann. She would approve his beautiful manners and be completely won by that Viennese charm. Aunt Margaret was astute. She would see, too, beneath the charm to the sincerity and warmth of the man.

'How is it you say in English? One penny for your thinking?'

'A penny for your thoughts!' Sally corrected him, laughing. 'I don't know that they are worth a penny, Johann. I was just telling myself how *nice* you are.'

'That is worth the great deal more than all money,' Johann replied gravely. 'That you should be my friend makes me rich in happiness.'

'And that goes for me, too,' Sally said softly.

It did not seem in the least wrong or untimely that he should choose this moment once more to take and hold her hand.

12

As Sally made up her face in preparation for the morning's work, she noticed how pale she was. The golden tan of the Austrian sunshine had completely vanished and there were dark shadows, not only due to city life, beneath her eyes.

Carefully applying the eye-liner to give the upward slant Mike favoured, Sally thought how strange a thing time was. A minute could seem an hour, an hour a minute. It was all of eight weeks since that fantastic holiday. Conversely, it hardly seemed more than a few months that she had last modelled for Mike before her accident. Coming back to the studio had been a strange experience, but when the first few unsettling days had gone by, it was almost as if she had never left. Now, having worked here for three weeks, she had fallen back into the old familiar routine as if there had been no break, no accident, nothing to interrupt the flow of their work.

Yet it had not been the same. Somehow she and Mike could not reach the same close understanding they had once shared and taken completely for granted. Now he was often irritable with her. At first she had mistaken this irritability for the well-remembered impatience he had always shown when he could not achieve exactly the pose or effect he wanted. She was used to it, and it did not disturb her too much. But as the days passed she began to realise that he was not just impatient — he was annoyed. She realised, too, that the fault was hers, not his. She could no longer pose for him properly, 'Turn your head the other way, Sally — not right, *left!*'

'Cup your chin in your hand, this way — so that your hand covers your cheek!'

'Bend your head a little — away from

the light. I want to accentuate your shoulders, not your face. Oh, for God's sake, Sally, have a little feeling for what I'm trying to do.'

Beneath the carefully applied make-up, Sally's face flushed at the memory of those words and others like them. How slow she had been to grasp Mike's meaning. It had taken days of frustrating failures before she realised that Mike wanted her to conceal the scarred side of her face from him, from the camera. She began to notice that he was pleased whenever she managed to cover her scar without his asking her to do so; that he only lost his temper and swore at her when she forgot. She began to notice that this applied even when he was not photographing her. He preferred to sit beside her rather than opposite her; to dance with his left cheek against her right cheek — opposite to the normal position. He encouraged her to wear her chiffon turbans once more; to set her hair so that it hung either side of her face in the most concealing way.

The realisation that he was still affected by her scar was so gradual that it was not so much a shock as a slowly realised pain. It began to affect her posing. She could no longer be natural but positioned herself stiffly, awkwardly. Mike, quite understandably, complained that she was hopelessly unnatural.

'What on earth's the matter with you, Sally? You're as stiff as a board. My God, girl, you *are* out of practice!'

'Give me time,' Sally had whispered, near to tears.

This morning she had arrived for work feeling more apprehensive than ever. Last night, when she left the studio to go home, Mike had torn up all the day's work and thrown it on the floor.

'A whole day wasted!' he had stormed. 'I'll never get anywhere like this. Why, even a novice could do better!'

The day had been equally trying,

equally disappointing for her, too. Stung to reply, she had flung back at him:

'It's your fault. You won't let me be natural. How can I slip into a natural pose when all the time you're worrying whether I'm going to show my scar. I hate you, I hate you!' she had added childishly and burst into tears.

Mike had stared at her for a long moment before he stepped over the torn rolls of film and took her in his arms.

'I'm sorry, Sal. It isn't that *I* mind, but you must see that nobody's going to want photographs of a model unless the face is . . . well, perfect. It doesn't have to be beautiful but it does have to be flawless.'

'I know, I know! But you said you could touch out the imperfections. When we talked in Austria about my modelling for you again it was you who said the scar didn't matter — that it barely showed!'

Mike had released her and left her

standing staring at his back as he went over to the window.

'I hadn't had a chance to take any shots then. I didn't realise the scar would show up the way it does on film. And it isn't just that, Sal. You're so taut and strung up. You can't seem to get the poses I want.'

'Maybe you'd better get another model!' Sally said quietly, feeling as if the bottom of her world had dropped away.

'Don't be silly. You know I want you. For pity's sake don't let's have temperament on top of everything else. Today's been bad enough without a scene to cap it. Forget it. Go home. Have a good night's sleep and we'll try again tomorrow.'

He seemed to have forgotten that they had arranged to go down the road to their favourite Italian restaurant for supper. She went back to the flat to spend a miserable evening alone. Bobbie was up north visiting Basil's family. Aunt Margaret had been going to come up to the flat on a visit, but she had had a nasty bout of 'flu the week before and thought it wiser to remain at home.

Sally had had a hot bath and gone to bed early but she had not been able to sleep. The sense of failure was agonising. It wasn't just that she was beginning to feel she was finished as a model, but that she was losing Mike's love, too. He had been so passionately adoring when they'd first returned from Austria. Nothing was too much trouble and he had even consented to go down to Aunt Margaret's for a weekend. The weekend had not been a success, though both Mike and Aunt Margaret had tried. Her aunt knew that they had become engaged and tried to be happy for Sally's sake, but somehow she and Mike always seemed to rub each other up the wrong way.

But on their return to London, they had gone to the studio for coffee and a night-cap and Mike had been everything she could ever want. Again and again he told her how much he loved her; how he couldn't wait to get married; how the thought of surviving the next three months living apart was too much to bear. She had felt the same way and been sorely tempted to bring forward the date of the wedding she had fixed with Aunt Margaret for early August.

They could have been married at once but Aunt Margaret wanted Sally to have a village church wedding and also, Johann was coming on the promised visit in July. It would be awkward for Sally, as Mike's wife, to escort Johann around England and act as hostess to him as she had promised.

'I don't mind waiting till August for the *wedding*,' Mike had argued pointedly. 'I just don't want to wait that long for you. I don't see why you can't move in here with me. Bobbie can find another flat-mate. I want to make love to you . . . '

Sally had refused. Much as she herself wanted Mike to make love to her, it seemed pointless to give in at this time with their wedding so near. Old fashioned though Mike thought her, she clung to her ideal of being a genuinely virgin bride. She did toy momentarily with the idea of putting Johann off; but she couldn't do it. She felt obligated to keep her promise and that was all there was to it. She knew from Johann's weekly letters how greatly he was looking forward to the visit. His train and boat tickets were already booked. Aunt Margaret was having the spare room redecorated for his arrival. No, not even for Mike would she disappoint him now. But the temptation was there. Over and over again, Mike begged her to anticipate the marriage. Always she refused, but her refusals only seemed to increase his ardour.

When had he stopped trying to persuade her to move in with him? Sally could not be sure. She realised that his attitude to her work was somehow affecting their personal relationship. He became more and more irritable; less and less lover-like; quicker to find fault; slower to praise. And quite suddenly, she was wretchedly and painfully aware that Mike never mentioned their wedding these days; that when she brought up the subject, he would turn it aside, saying:

'First things first, Sally. Let's try that beach shot again. Slip into your bikini, will you? We'll see if we can't do a bit better this time.'

Carefully, Sally applied her lipstick. Her hands trembled as she filled in the outlines. The lipstick smudged. Clenching her teeth, she scrubbed off the paint and began again. But now her lips, too, were trembling. She felt on the brink of tears.

'Hurry up, Sally. I haven't all day!'

Mike's voice, impatient, from the studio, reached her clearly. Sally sat back, staring at her reflection, trying to get back a measure of self-control. She knew in advance that she wouldn't be able to pose this morning the way Mike wanted. Just occasionally things went well and he was pleased, but the way she felt now, a bundle of nerves, she knew the day would be disastrous. What point was there in going in there to try? Better surely to explain to Mike that she didn't feel too well and would rather not work that morning.

'Are you coming or aren't you, Sal?'

He came into the tiny bathroom where she was making up and stared down at her, his eyes thoughtful.

'No, I'm not coming, Mike. I can't do it. I just can't . . . I . . . I don't feel too good!'

Mike's face remained inscrutable, showing neither disappointment nor surprise.

'Oh, well, if that's how you feel, I suppose there's not much point in trying to work.'

She swung round and held out her hands to him in sudden appeal.

'Let's give it a break this morning, Mike. Let's do something quite different . . . something silly, meaningless, something that'll be fun. Let's go to Regent's Park or go to the Zoo, or . . . '

'Darling, don't be silly. I've got to get these proofs off today. They're late already, you know that.'

'Mike, please! We can work this afternoon. I think if we could have a few hours together just . . . just doing something unimportant, it would relax me and this afternoon I'd be all right. Please, darling?'

He dropped his eyes and felt in his pocket for a packet of cigarettes. She watched as he lit up and inhaled deeply for a minute or two.

'Better not!' he said. 'But you run along if you feel like it. I've probably been overworking you. A break will do you good. Tell you what, we'll meet up for dinner at Castoni's. How about that?'

Her hands fell to her sides. It wasn't what she had wanted, but she could see that Mike's mood did not match her own. He wanted to work.

'I'll reprint some of those culotte

shots I took last week. Maybe one of them will be all right. Anyway, it's my worry, not yours. You run along, darling, and make the most of the sunshine.'

He bent and lightly kissed the top of her head. She rose to her feet and put her arms round him, lifting her mouth for his kiss. He kissed her lightly, without passion. She could not have accused him of unresponsiveness and yet she felt rejected, unhappier than ever.

'Love me?' she asked, her voice carefully light, casual.

'Of course, my sweet. What a silly question from a very silly little girl.'

'Mike, I'm not a girl. I'm a woman. I love you very much. I . . . I've the feeling lately that things aren't right between us. You'd say, wouldn't you? You'd be honest if . . . if . . . '

'Now, Sally, don't go all emotional on me — not at ten o'clock in the morning. Of course I'd be honest with you and say if anything was wrong. I know the work hasn't been going so well, but it's natural you should have got a bit out of practice with all that time off work. I've been pushing you too hard . . . or maybe you've been trying too hard. It'll all come right.'

'You do really believe that?' she asked. 'If I thought you had confidence in me, darling, I think I'd regain some confidence, too. I seem to have lost it all.' She turned away and sat down at the dressing table and began to remove her modelling make-up and to replace it with her own daytime face. Mike remained standing behind her, watching her.

'You really are beautiful!' he said, more to himself than to her. 'Your bone structure is extraordinary, Sally. I've never found anyone else with quite that perfection of foundation. Even the . . . the scar can't hide it.'

Involuntarily Sally's hands went to her cheek.

'It still bothers you, doesn't it, Mike? Don't shake your head. I know it does, but I'll be having that last operation soon. Then it will not be noticeable. The surgeon promised me.'

Mike drew heavily on his cigarette and let out a cloud of smoke.

'Do you think it might be sensible to give the modelling a rest until after . . . well, after the operation?' he said slowly.

Sally's cheeks filled with colour.

'Oh, Mike!' she whispered. 'I don't want to give it up, but if you think . . . '

'It's up to you, of course. I just got the impression you were getting bored with it!' Mike broke in. 'Naturally I'm not going back on anything I said. Some of the work we've done lately has been marvellous. It's just that we do seem to have to throw away an awful lot before we hit on the one really good one. In the old days it was the other way round.'

'Yes, I know! I'll do whatever you think best. I . . . I don't *want* to give it up but . . . ' Her voice trailed into silence. Mike moved away from her, shrugging his shoulders.

'It's your decision,' he said again. 'Think about it and let me know.'

Sally completed her dressing and followed him into the studio. He was leafing through a selection of photographs, absorbed in what he was doing. She longed with a painful intensity to go across the room and hold that dark head against her breast; to feel his arms go round her, drawing her close; to hear his voice telling her that it wasn't the photographs which were in the least important. What mattered was them — him and her; their love; their approaching marriage. But what kind of a marriage would it be if she couldn't work for him? She would be living here in the studio with him. There was only this one big room and the bedroom next door. If he engaged another model, they would all be on top of one another. Mike liked to work at all hours, depending on his mood. Sometimes he worked on, if the model was willing, until midnight. They would have no privacy, no life of their own. Always there would be a third person in their lives for Mike chose to work ninety per cent of the time with one girl only.

Sally turned away and with a casual 'Goodbye, darling, see you later!' left the studio and went out on to the sunlit pavement. She ignored the buses and began to walk in the direction of the park. The sky was a brilliant clear blue — not quite as deep but reminiscent of the sky above the white mountains in Austria. It was a day to be out of doors, preferably in the country. It was a shame Mike wouldn't come with her. The studio with its artificial lights and heat was no compensation for the soft golden warmth of the sunshine.

Half an hour later, Sally was sitting on a bench in Regent's Park. She had brought some sandwiches and a carton of milk and was intending to have a solitary picnic lunch. But she was only a few minutes before someone addressed her.

'Sally Marsden, isn't it?'

She looked up to see Jess's dark eyes smiling down at her.

'Why, Jess! What on earth are you doing here?'

'Or you?' Jess said, laughing as she sat down on the bench beside Sally. 'My first appointment isn't until two. I'm working freelance now — for an agency. It's rather fun. One day one photographer, one day another. I find I prefer it to working for one person only. There's more variety.'

Mike's name lay unspoken between them. Sally broke the ice. She told Jess she had gone back to work for him and suddenly found herself telling her what a failure she had turned out to be on this second attempt.

'I'm worse than I was when I first started!' she said ruefully. 'A complete amateur. No wonder Mike gets fed up with me!'

Jess stared at the younger girl thoughtfully.

'I suppose I'm not really surprised to

253

hear you went back to him. Knowing Mike, I thought it wouldn't take him long to persuade you. I knew he wanted you back, of course. Without in any way belittling you, Sally, I never quite understood why. Do you mind my saying that? I don't intend anything derogatory to you. Frankly I think you're far more beautiful than you were before your accident.'

Sally smiled.

'I don't mind you talking this way. To tell you the truth, I've often wondered myself. I know Mike hates my scar. He tries to hide it, but it still bothers him. Perhaps he realised how much I wanted to model for him again and let me do so to make me happy.'

Jess's face lost its smile. Her eyes were thoughtful and she hesitated a moment before she said:

'At the risk of offending you, Sally, I can't believe that Mike ever had an altruistic motive in his life. You must know as well as I do that unselfishness isn't one of Mike's plus signs . . . rather the reverse.'

Sally looked at the dark girl gently.

'You're bitter about him, Jess, and I understand why. He . . . he didn't behave very well to you in Zürs, did he?'

Jess shrugged.

'Oh, I got over that. I wasn't really in love with him. I just thought I was. Mike has that ability to mesmerise any woman he wants. And he did want me, Sally, for a while. He . . . he let me believe he would marry me. I moved into the studio with him, more fool I. Does that shock you?'

'N . . . no!' Sally said untruthfully. Yet it did surprise her. Mike had given no hint that he had had an affair with Jess; that she had moved in to live with him. He'd inferred their relationship was only a casual one.

'I'm not telling you this to make you feel bad . . . or to get my own back on Mike,' Jess continued. 'I don't know or care what Mike has told you about me

— but I think you should know the truth. You see, Sally, you may be like me, mesmerised. I'd hate you to be tricked the way I was.'

'We're going to get married,' Sally said softly. 'In August. The date's fixed.'

Jess's eyebrows shot up as if Sally's words really surprised her. Then she covered Sally's hand with her own and said warmly:

'I'm happy for you, if it's what you want. Perhaps I was wrong and he really does love you. I hope so.'

'I hope so, too!' Sally said, laughing to cover the fact that she felt a chill run down her spine. *Did Mike love her? Had he ever really loved her? Was she about to marry a man who didn't know the real meaning of the word?*

Unwilling to follow her own train of thought, Sally quickly changed the subject.

'Do you remember the Austrian ski guide I met in Austria?' she asked. 'He's coming over in July. Would you like to meet him again? He's coming to stay with us — with my aunt and me in Sussex. Perhaps you would be able to come down for a weekend?'

'I'd love to!' Jess said. 'Johann was nice. *Très sympatique*, if I remember rightly. As a matter of fact, I thought him quite charming. I had the impression he was halfway to being in love with you himself.'

To Sally's surprise, she found herself telling Jess about Johann. She had not told anyone else he had all but said he loved her, not Bobbie, certainly not Mike and not even Aunt Margaret. But it was all too easy to confide in Jess. She liked her; felt they had a lot in common. She would be happy to have Jess as a close friend.

Soon the two girls were sharing Sally's meagre lunch.

'Better for our figures if we don't eat too much!' Jess said, laughing.

They chatted easily until it was time for Jess to leave for her appointment.

'Come with me, Sally,' she begged. 'Maybe the agency will have something for you. It might do you good to do a job for someone else. Do come!'

But Sally shook her head.

'I think I'll go back to the studio,' she said. 'I feel so much better now. I think I could work well this afternoon. I'll surprise Mike. Meeting you, talking and laughing the way we have done, has made me feel a new person. We'll see each other again, won't we, Jess?'

They made a date for the following day and Sally walked happily back to the studio. The door was locked when she arrived, but she had her own key and let herself in. Mike must have gone out for lunch.

She went into the studio and switched on the lights. As usual Mike had left the place hopelessly untidy. Methodically she began to put things back in their proper places. She worked systematically for ten minutes on props and then began to tidy the mass of photographs on Mike's table. They were nearly all of herself, but suddenly her eye was caught by a different face

— one she didn't know. It was small, bony, very young-looking. The girl couldn't have been more than sixteen.

Sally studied the proofs more closely, sitting down at the table to do so. The background seemed familiar; it was the beach scene she and Mike had been working on all last week. It was for a magazine doing a feature on holiday clothes. Her eyes went back to the model. The clothes, too, were the same.

Her hands were trembling now. Sally turned over the proofs to look at the backs. Mike's date stamp was clearly marked. May 19th. So he had taken them last Thursday.

Her mind went back to the Thursday. Where had she, Sally, been? She remembered without difficulty. That was the day Aunt Margaret had 'flu and she'd telephoned Mike to say she'd be unable to come to work as she had to go down to Sussex to make sure her aunt was being properly cared for. These pictures must have been taken whilst she was in the country.

Sally put them back on the table, covering them with her trembling hands. Her thoughts were in chaos. There was nothing wrong in Mike taking those photographs — nothing wrong at all, but *why hadn't he told her?* Why keep it a secret? Why do it behind her back? If he hadn't been happy with the ones of herself, he had only to say so. And how had he found this girl? Phoned an agency? Or had he known her some time? Had he used her before?

Sally never looked in the magazine he took pictures for. There was always a delay of weeks or months between submission of the pictures and printing. By the time the magazine was published, she and Mike were working on something else, and unless she happened to come upon one by accident, she never saw herself in print. For all she knew, all the pictures Mike had taken of her since she had started to work again had been relegated to the waste-paper basket and pictures of this girl substituted instead for the magazines.

Sally felt her cheeks go hot with shame. If Mike had cheated her in this way, it must have been from pity. He hadn't wanted to tell her to her face that she was no good. He hadn't wanted to hurt her. It was the only possible explanation. He could not have been training a young girl behind her back ready to step into her shoes without giving her some idea of the truth unless it was from a desire to save her pride. It was too dishonest — too unthinkable.

She sat there, lost in thought, unmoving. She did not even hear Mike's key turn in the door. It was not until she heard him speak that she looked up to find him standing there, staring at her and at the pictures beneath her hands, his eyes angry, his face pale.

'I'd no idea,' he said icily, 'that you'd be coming back to spy.'

13

Sally's face went a dark red.

'I wasn't spying!' she cried. 'I came back to work. When I found you weren't here I thought I'd tidy up for you. Oh, Mike . . . ' her voice became pleading, 'why didn't you tell me you'd been using another model?'

Mike turned away uneasily.

'I thought you'd be annoyed,' he said sulkily.

She stared at his back thoughtfully.

'Who is she?' she asked at last.

Mike shrugged.

'Oh, just a kid from one of the agencies — calls herself Candy and wants me to make her into another Twiggy.'

His voice was carefully casual. Sally picked up the photographs and looked at them again, trying to see them objectively.

'Have you used her often, Mike? I *wish* you'd told me about her.'

He swung round and stared down at her like a sulky schoolboy.

'You'd have kicked up an awful scene if I *had* told you. You'd have gone all remorseful and said you weren't good enough and all that nonsense!'

'Wouldn't it be true?' Sally's voice was surprisingly calm, although her heart was hammering violently and she knew her hands were still trembling. 'I'm no good as a model any more, Mike, and we might both just as well face it. I'm too self-conscious and I know it. Why don't you admit it, too?'

Mike seemed surprised by her quiet tone and calm manner. He relaxed and came towards her, putting a hand on her shoulder.

'Well, we have been finding things a bit tricky lately, haven't we, my sweet? You are too self-conscious. Maybe it would be a good plan to give it a break for a while. Perhaps we've both been trying too hard. A month or two off work could make all the difference.'

Sally had not realised until then that she had been holding her breath. Now she exhaled slowly.

'I'm glad you haven't given me up as altogether useless,' she said shakily. 'Darling, you do honestly think I'll get back on form in a little while? I don't seem to have any self-confidence left. I . . . it's my face, of course . . . my scar. Maybe after the operation . . . that's scheduled for October . . . then when that's all over there'll be nothing showing at all and I won't have anything to be nervous about.'

Mike bent down and touched the top of her head with his lips.

'You're a wonderful girl, Sally. I've misjudged you. I thought you'd be furious about Candy. I should have told you about her but I was so afraid you'd be upset. I thought you might start imagining the girl herself meant something to me. It's purely a working partnership. You do believe that, don't you?'

Sally smiled.

'Yes, of course. She's only a kid. How old? Sixteen? You are an old silly if you imagined I'd suspect you of cradle-snatching. Oh, Mike, I feel so much better now we've had it all out. I've known for weeks I wasn't making good — that you weren't happy with the results of our work. I was afraid to admit it. It seems so silly now. I suppose I felt it would affect our personal relationship in some way. I just couldn't bear it if you stopped loving me.'

He drew her out of the chair and put his arms around her. 'Of course I still love you. Whatever put such a doubt into your silly little head?'

Their kiss was long and passionate. Both were breathing deeply when at last Mike released her and said huskily:

'I don't think *you* really love *me*, Sally. If you did, you wouldn't hold back the way you do. Stay here with me tonight. Or let me come to the flat. Bobbie's away, isn't she? It's a heaven-sent opportunity. You've made such a 'thing' about it darling. Can't you see it's just a tiny step to take. I love you and you say you love me. Prove it.'

Sally cupped his face in her hands and looked deeply into his eyes. They were feverishly bright, demanding. She wanted to say yes — to give him everything in the world he wanted. Some tiny instinct deep within her told her that she could not be a hundred per cent sure of his love; that he might be growing a little tired of her, impatient with her. Perhaps if she gave herself to him fully, he would be as completely hers as she was his.

'Say yes, darling. I love you so much. It's all so crazy when we're going to be married in a few weeks anyway. No one would know, and I promise to take the greatest care of you. Sally, darling . . . '

He was kissing her again, his hands on her body tempting, demanding, possessive. She felt herself weakening. Was it such a big step after all? Wasn't Mike right when he said it was crazy to deny him what he wanted. In a few weeks' time she would be his wife. What could it matter if . . .

Suddenly Jess's words sprang to her mind.

'I'd hate you to be mesmerised the way I was . . . I'd hate you to be tricked . . . he made me believe he'd marry me . . .'

But that was Jess. Mike had never loved Jess. He loved her, Sally. He was going to marry her . . .

'No, Mike!' The words came almost involuntarily. 'I don't want to. I'd rather wait. I . . .'

'You don't trust me. You think I don't really love you. Is that it?' He looked angry, resentful, thwarted, as he let go of her and walked away across the studio.

'Darling, don't be hurt, please. Try to understand. I want it as much as you do, but not this way . . . I want it all to be perfect when it does happen. This way seems all wrong and it doesn't prove anything . . . just that we haven't any self-control. I know that sounds priggish, but we've waited so long — a few more weeks can't hurt either of us. Please, darling, try to understand.'

'Sorry, but I don't! I just understand that you don't need me the way I need you — you never did. I'm beginning to wonder if you're one of those women who basically dislike sex — frigid. You don't look it but that doesn't necessarily mean anything.'

Sally's cheeks were scarlet, her voice indignant as she flared back at him:

'That is a hateful remark, Mike, and not worthy of you. If you really think that way, then I've been sadly mistaken about you.'

He came back to her then, his face apologetic.

'I'm sorry, darling. Of course I didn't mean it. I'm just terribly hurt. A man doesn't like to feel himself unwanted that way.'

Now she, too, softened. Her arms went round him and she hugged him childishly, almost maternally.

'I do want you, I do! You're the most

attractive man I've ever met. I love you, Mike. I've always loved you. You have to believe it. You do believe it, don't you?'

He allowed her to kiss him, plead with him. She looked very beautiful, bright-eyed, eager, loving, flushed with emotion. He wanted her very badly. Her rejection of him renewed all the old desire to possess her. She was not like the new kid, Candy — all angles and bones and gawkiness. Sally was essentially feminine — a curved, soft, beautifully rounded woman . . . the woman he wanted and couldn't get. Not without marriage. All the others — Jess, Candy and those before, had fallen willingly enough. Sally was the only one who always said 'no' yet whose love was deepest. She was *too* deep for him really. His nature was much more superficial than hers. Sometimes the intensity of her feelings overpowered him; made him feel inadequate. He knew that he did not love her in the same way. He desired her . . . and her virginity was a constant nagging challenge to him.

He wished now that he hadn't telephoned Candy to come round to the studio at three o'clock. The child was brash and inexperienced. She might easily let something slip. If Sally knew he'd been fooling around with her, he might lose Sally altogether. Her standards were very different from his own. He saw no great virtue in faithfulness for its own sake. Not that he felt Sally had any right to blame him if he found consolation elsewhere. Maybe if she . . .

'I can't make you change your mind — about tonight?'

She met his gaze levelly.

'I don't want to, Mike!' she said simply, regretfully.

'Well, at least let me come round and see you. I promise not to let things go any further than you want. We'll have supper at Castoni's as we planned and go back to your flat for coffee.'

For a moment Sally hesitated. She

had deliberately not asked Mike round while Bobbie was away, knowing what a temptation it would be to them both to have the place entirely to themselves. But this was different. Mike knew how she felt; he'd promised to keep himself in control. If she refused to allow him to come to the flat now, he'd think she didn't trust him.

'All right, darling,' she said. 'I'll go round and tidy up a bit — I left the place upside down this morning in my hurry to get to work. I overslept.'

She did not add that she had hardly slept at all until the early hours; that she had lain awake worrying about her work; her face; Mike's reactions to that coming day. She was so easily hurt when he was angry and impatient with her. Now that strain would be a thing of the past. She wasn't going to try to model for him again until after the last operation.

She left the studio just before three o'clock and took a bus home in a far happier frame of mind than she began the morning. She would have a bath and a rest when she had tidied up, so that she looked fresh and beautiful for Mike that evening. Her mirror did not throw back a reflection she particularly cared for at the moment. The shadows beneath her eyes were far too dark and deeply etched. There were tiny frown lines on her forehead and she was very pale. Somehow the sun-tan she had acquired in Austria had diminished the scar so that out there she had almost forgotten its existence. Now it seemed to show painfully clearly even beneath her London make-up. She was almost as conscious of it as she had been when she went to Austria.

Bathed and relaxed, lying beneath the duvet, Sally allowed her mind to wander. As so often, her thoughts went back to that wonderful ski-ing holiday. It had had its moments of crisis! she thought dreamily. Fortunately Johann's kindness in lending the money to pay for the broken drums had averted disaster and the last week had been almost as perfect as the first. She had spent most of the remaining days with Mike, of course, but she had managed to get out for her daily ski lesson with Johann, and there had been the last-but-one night out dancing with him. He'd proved the perfect companion as always; considerate, restful, easy to be with after those hours with a restless Mike cooped up because of his ankle.

Sally smiled. Mike was such a little boy in some ways. He was so easily bored; wanting entertaining all the time. Even when he hobbled downstairs and could sit out in a chair in the sun, he soon lost interest in watching the skiers, although he had a wonderful view of the nursery slopes and there was always something going on. But then he didn't ski — in fact, he didn't enjoy any outdoor sports, so it was understandable that he should grow tired of watching other people. He only really became himself when they were in a friendly group at the bar or if they were alone in his room. How impatiently he had pleaded with her then to make love. She had needed all her self-control to refuse him. She loved him so much and wanted to make him happy. Yet she had said 'no' just as she had said 'no' this afternoon in the studio.

Half asleep, Sally wondered at herself. It wasn't just her upbringing, although Aunt Margaret had been conventional enough. It was something Aunt Margaret had once said to her:

'I don't advise you to refuse because I think virginity itself is important, but because I am convinced that sex outside marriage never yet made any girl truly happy! You see, darling, a girl is much more deeply involved than a man — every emotion is called into play if she's your kind of woman. Sex for its own sake isn't enough . . .'

Sally had thought a lot about it. She had listened to other girls discussing it; those who had and those who hadn't. She had seen Aunt Margaret's warning fulfilled when her best friend fell in love and, weeks later, tried to kill herself when the man walked out on her. She'd seen another friend radiant with happiness on her return from her honeymoon; heard her say with fervour how *glad* she was she had waited. She, herself, had been glad she'd held back when her engagement to Mike had been broken off after the accident. It didn't alter matters that they had come together again. She knew that if she had belonged fully to Mike in those early days, the break would have been even more agonising than it was.

She felt happy in her decision and determined that tonight she would find a way to make Mike understand.

She loved him and he loved her. That was the only really important thing.

Relaxed at last, Sally fell asleep.

14

Aunt Margaret sat in the one comfortable armchair and surveyed the young girl sitting cross-legged at her feet. The child looked so young, she thought, suddenly conscious of her own grey hair and thickening figure. She was forty-six — only four years off fifty! Now she felt old seeing Bobbie's youthful coltishness which contrasted so surprisingly with the worldly wisdom coming from her wide, generous mouth. The child spoke like a woman of the world, and yet Margaret Marsden knew she was only a year older than her niece, Sally. If the two girls were women, then she was an old, old woman, she thought ruefully.

But she had not come to the flat to think about herself. Her life was settled in a comfortable familiar pattern, moving at a slow not-unpleasant pace tucked away as she was in her little Sussex village, tending her garden in the summer, dabbling with her pottery in the winter. The quiet, uneventful days were broken pleasantly but spasmodically by Sally's visits.

Sally! It was her niece she was so worried about. Sally had not been down for almost a month and whenever she spoke to her on the telephone, her excuses for not coming sounded more and more improbable. It was not like Sally to be evasive. She had always confided in her aunt and they were as close, if not closer, than most mothers and daughters.

Margaret Marsden had little doubt that Sally's fiancé was responsible for the rift between them, if you could call a total absence of any contact a rift. Mike had never liked her, nor she him. If she could have found any valid reason to prevent Sally marrying him, she would not have hesitated to expose him. But she knew Sally loved him; none knew better how terribly Sally had suffered when he'd backed off after the accident. How she had despised that young man in those days! Oh, Sally had sought to excuse him even then and now that they were together again, would not hear a word against his behaviour at that time. It was *her* fault, she reiterated. Mike had only carried out her wishes as he had truly believed them to be. She had only herself to blame . . .

It interested and intrigued Margaret Marsden to hear, for the first time today, that Sally's young flat companion, Bobbie, liked Mike as little as she did herself, and trusted him even less.

Margaret Marsden was far too principled a person to have questioned Bobbie behind Sally's back. She had fully intended to talk to Sally herself but when she had arrived, it was to find her niece out and Bobbie only too pleased to welcome her and pour out her own misgivings to an older sympathetic ear.

'Sally might not like me talking to

you this way, but I feel I have to, for *her* sake!' Bobbie had burst out over their shared pot of tea. 'She's unhappy. I know it and I guessed she hadn't told you because when I suggested she did so, she replied that she wasn't going to have you worried and upset, too. She knows how fond of her you are and said you'd be sure to try to make her break with Mike. That's the whole trouble, Miss Marsden, she can't bring herself to leave him. She still loves him.'

Bit by bit, Margaret Marsden heard the facts. Sally had been seeing less and less of Mike. Night after night, she waited by the phone for him to ring but he could never be relied upon to do so. Often, when he did telephone, it was to make some excuse why he couldn't see her or meet her as arranged. Sally hadn't been working for him for some weeks. He had another model — a young beginner called Candy. Sally had confided in Bobbie that she was afraid Mike might be taking more than a professional interest in the girl.

'Then Sally should have enough pride to break off their engagement,' Margaret Marsden said, sighing. 'Frankly, none of this surprises me. I never trusted him. If it does have to happen, I thank God it is now and not after the wedding.'

Bobbie poured out two more cups of tea and sighed deeply.

'It isn't as simple as that. Sally is making excuses for Mike. She says he is an artist and therefore incapable of dissociating himself from the models he works with. He needs to have some kind of personal contact if he is to get the best out of a model — an understanding which Mike apparently calls an '*entente*'. Sally seems to believe that he still loves her as much as ever, but that he hasn't the time to show it any more. She says it'll be different after they are married.'

'I dare say it would!' Margaret Marsden said dryly. 'The man can hardly have his model and his wife after working hours.'

Bobbie nodded, her red curls falling across her face.

'I know that. So does Mike. He's been hinting about postponing the wedding until after he's finished a series he's working on for some new magazine. He told Sally last week that he simply couldn't get away for a honeymoon until Christmas. Frankly, I don't like the situation at all, Miss Marsden. I think he might let her down again and I couldn't bear that for her. She loves him quite desperately.'

'Does she? Or is it just a question of thinking she loves him? I sometimes wonder. He has a strange hold over her. But then she was very young indeed when she met him, and she has never looked at another boy. I wish she had. At least then she could make some comparisons.'

For a moment silence filled the room. Then Bobbie said:

'She did notice Johann — the Austrian boy. She liked him. I think if Mike hadn't turned up when he did, she might even have fallen in love with him. I could have cried my eyes out the night I knew Mike was there in Zürs.'

'You know Johann is coming to stay with us next week?'

Bobbie looked up, grinning.

'Yes, I do, and I can't tell you how much I'm pinning on his visit. He's crazy about Sally — or he was. He'd do anything for her. I'm hoping Mike will show up a very poor second when she sees Johann again.'

Margaret Marsden sighed.

'Unfortunately a girl in love is frequently blind to the virtues of other men, just as she is blind to the faults of the man she loves.'

'Oh, I'm not!' Bobbie replied cheerfully. 'I know Basil's moody and he has a frightful temper and he's not all that madly intelligent. But I don't really care. I love him *in spite* of his faults. We're engaged, you know. It happened when I went up to visit his people. His Mum's a darling, and they were all ever so nice to me. I'm lucky, aren't I, Miss

Marsden? Everything's going so smoothly for me. I just *wish* Sally could be happy, too. She seems too miserable. Love ought to make you happy, oughtn't it? I don't believe in that old saying that the path of true love never runs smooth.'

'No, nor do I. And I hope you'll be very happy always, Bobbie. Sally has spoken of you so often with such affection. You've been a wonderful friend to her.'

'I've tried!' Bobbie said, sighing, 'but there isn't much I can do about this Mike of hers. I'd like to give him a piece of my mind, but, of course, Sally won't let me near him. She knows I don't like him. I can't understand how a beautiful girl like Sal can let a man push her around the way he does. She ought to be pushing him around. But just when I think even the long-suffering Sally is going to turn, he takes her out somewhere and tells her she's wonderful and she's back where she was the day before, making excuses for him because he doesn't do it all the time.'

'You don't think he's having an affair with the other girl — this Candy?' Miss Marsden said bluntly.

Bobbie shrugged.

'Could be! I wouldn't put it past him. I wouldn't put anything past him. Frankly, I think that's what holds him to Sal — she won't sleep with him. She must be the only girl he's wanted who has refused, so I suppose that has the fascination of the unusual, especially as he can hardly doubt she loves him. He probably doesn't understand it and is as much intrigued as annoyed. I dunno. I'm just guessing really. I know there was a terrible scene here while I was away visiting Basil. Sally had him back here and he refused to leave. In the end, Sally got him out of the flat and locked the door and our neighbours heard him banging on it and asking to be let in again. It might have been an amusing story except that Sally was so upset. Apparently he'd promised to behave and then accused her of letting him down. She swears she made it quite clear that he couldn't stay all night and that she wasn't going to give way. I suppose he just didn't believe she could resist him. One up to Sally, I say.'

'Then you think she's right — not to give way?' Margaret Marsden asked curiously. This young girl's point of view interested her. One read and heard such extraordinary stories of the young these days. Yet when one met them, they were often surprisingly moral in their outlook.

'Too true!' Bobbie said without hesitation. 'If that was all he was after, then he'd soon get bored when the novelty had worn off, and then where would she be? I think having sex with a man makes the relationship much deeper, much more difficult to break off, much harder to readjust to someone else. I'd have to be terribly, terribly sure of a man before I did — and then, if you're sure of him and sure you love him, what's to stop you getting married? That's why Basil and I are getting married soon. We're both sure and we don't want to wait. We want each other too much to go in for a long engagement. We're going to live with his Mum for a bit — until we can afford a flat of our own.'

'And suppose Mike really does love Sally and we've misjudged him? You still think she's right to refuse?'

'Sure I do!' Bobbie again replied instantly. 'If he feels that way, he should be begging her to hurry up the wedding. Instead of which he seems to be quite happy to sit back while she plays hostess to another man — to Johann. Whatever made him agree to such a thing? I wouldn't — if it were Basil and some Austrian girl he'd met. Johann's a very good-looking guy and you'd have thought Mike would be really jealous. Sally, of course, says Mike knows he can trust her so he doesn't have to be jealous. He knows he's got her where he wants her is more like it!'

Sally's aunt nodded thoughtfully. Bobbie's thoughts might pour out in a flood of opinion, but they were perfectly logical. She, herself, had been glad when Sally told her she did not intend to get married at once. She would have welcomed any delay in the wedding. But now, thinking back, she could see that it was unnatural. Two young people in love — who had once been practically engaged and who had newly found each other again — it would have been far more natural if they had been as impatient for marriage as this young girl and her Basil.

'In my opinion,' Bobbie said slowly as she jumped to her feet to clear away the tea-tray, ' . . . Mike doesn't want to get married at all. He just wants Sally and that's different. I don't think he's the marrying type. He isn't even really Sally's type. They are about as opposite as two people could be. They can't have a single interest in common apart from the camera . . . and that's another thing I could kill him for. He's brought back

287

all Sal's phobias about her scar. She was almost over that obsession when we came back from Austria. Then something happened — I don't know what, and she started trying to hide her face again. It was to do with the photographs Mike was taking — the scar showed up and Mike kept telling her to keep that side of her profile away from the camera. It got so she couldn't pose naturally any more. Now she thinks she's lost her ability to be a model . . . or at least until she's rid of the last traces of the accident.'

'Yes, I noticed a change in her — a setback, when I last saw her,' Margaret Marsden said. 'It worried me, too. I didn't realise Mike was behind it. How cruel!'

'Well, he probably didn't mean it,' Bobbie replied. 'I dare say he was more thoughtless than anything else — insensitive, if you like. He probably didn't realise what he was doing to her. I don't think he realises it any time he hurts her or he couldn't do it. What to him is mere casualness to her is defection. I wish I never had to see her hanging on the end of that phone again! It was different when she went to the studio every day to work. Now she doesn't get to see him unless he takes her out or comes here to see her. I expect she's gone back to the studio with him now. They were lunching together and she'd hoped he was going to take the afternoon off, but he said he had to work at the last minute. I heard Sal say on the phone that if he didn't mind she'd drop in and watch him working. I'm sure she would be home now if she'd known you were coming.'

'I came on the spur of the moment,' the older woman said. 'I had a feeling something was very wrong and I thought I might find out more if I came unexpectedly. I didn't want to give Sally time to prepare a lot of defences. I would never force a confidence, but it isn't like her to shut me out. We've always been so close.'

'She doesn't talk to me either, any

more,' Bobbie admitted ruefully. 'She's very bright and chatty and cheerful, but I hear her crying in the night. The one time I did try to have it out with her, she told me very politely to mind my own business.'

Margaret Marsden sat back, squaring her shoulders.

'My mind is made up,' she said quietly. 'I'm not going home this evening until I've seen Sally, and I'm not leaving without having made at least one attempt to find out what's wrong.'

Bobbie nodded.

'I'll push off to the cinema so you can have the place to yourselves,' she said. 'I hope you succeed, Miss Marsden, and most of all I hope you'll be able to put things right. I can't. And I have the feeling that if anyone can, it'll be you.'

Bobbie went off to change out of her work clothes, but before she could leave the flat, a key turned in the lock and Sally came in. Bobbie, dressed now to go out, stood beside Miss Marsden staring at her friend, open-mouthed. Far from seeing the dejected, unhappy girl they had expected, Sally was radiant. She ran to her aunt and flung her arms round her, hugging her.

'Darling, what a wonderful surprise — a kind of bonus on the end of a wonderful day. Why didn't you tell me you were coming? Has Bobbie given you tea? Are you going out, Bobbie? What a shame — we could all have supper together. You'll stay, won't you, Aunt Margaret?'

Sally looked beautiful. Her huge green eyes were shining with happiness, her cheeks flushed and her fair hair windblown.

'Mike and I have been in Regent's Park,' she said, throwing herself down on the settee and kicking off her shoes, stretching her toes luxuriously. 'It was so lovely — all the birds singing and the flowers too beautiful for words. It's been a wonderful day, hasn't it?'

Bobbie carefully avoided Miss Marsden's eye. She felt totally nonplussed.

She had not seen Sally like this in weeks — not, in fact, since Austria.

'Tell us about it, darling,' Margaret Marsden said gently.

Sally snuggled herself more comfortably into the cushions and sighed.

'Oh, well, Mike and I had lunch together first at Castoni's — that's our favourite eating place near the studio. Well, Mike was supposed to be working after lunch and I'd said I'd go round and watch him but Mike suddenly decided in the middle of lunch to play hookey! 'It's far too nice a day to be indoors,' he said. 'Let's go somewhere!' It was such a surprise. Mike's not a walker and I nearly fell down when he suggested we went for a walk in the park.'

She jumped up and paced round the room like an excited schoolgirl and then flumped down on the floor at her aunt's feet and leant her head against her knees.

'It was gorgeous, Aunt Margaret — too hot to walk so we lay under a huge chestnut tree, my head in Mike's lap and talked and talked.'

'About your wedding?' Margaret Marsden asked.

'Well no, as a matter of fact. Let's see! We talked about Austria, of course, and Mike wanted to know all the places we're planning to take Johann. And then we talked about Jess — that's the girl who used to model for him. I met her once since Austria . . . but that's getting off the point. Oh, we talked about people and Mike's future as a photographer. He means to go to the very top, and I'm sure he will. He's terribly ambitious. He's met someone fairly high up in society who's taking an interest in him — he couldn't tell me who because it's all rather hush-hush at the moment, but if he can get commissioned to take studio shots of them, he thinks it'll be the start of really big things.'

Bobbie and Miss Marsden listened, each in their separate way following the same trend of thought. There had appeared no reason as yet for Sally's happiness. Neither the wedding nor their honeymoon nor their future had been discussed — only Mike and *his* future.

'Of course,' Sally was saying dreamily, 'Mike's terribly jealous because I'll be spending so much time in the next fortnight with Johann. He kept saying he was sure I'd find him as attractive as I did in Austria. In a way I am looking forward to seeing Johann again, but I can't help wishing he weren't coming just now when Mike and I . . . ' she broke off, her voice suddenly uncertain.

'When Mike and you . . . ?' her aunt prompted gently.

Sally averted her face. When she spoke it was in a deliberately casual voice.

'Oh, there've been odd times lately when we seem to have drifted apart a bit. It's only because I'm not modelling for him now and he's been so busy . . . nothing *serious*.' She jumped up, suddenly restless and fussed round her aunt, apologising for not having been down to see her, making plans for the following week.

When Margaret Marsden finally left to catch her train from Victoria, it was with mixed feelings. Her talk with Bobbie had been enlightening. But for that insight into Sally's life recently, she might have been taken in by today's radiance. As it was, she could see all too clearly how precarious Sally's happiness was. One did not have to be very astute to understand why Mike had suddenly taken Sally off to the park. He hadn't wanted her in the studio with the other girl around. Morever, the older woman thought as she settled herself into a compartment on the train home, she had not liked the way Mike had referred to Johann's visit — almost as if he were *hoping* Sally would find her Austrian boyfriend attractive. She could not dispel the fear that Mike hoped Sally would release him from a prospective marriage he no longer desired.

'My poor Sally!' she thought. It was awful to suspect that soon that happy, glowing young face was to be clouded with disappointment. But at the same time, Margaret Marsden could not prevent herself hoping her premonitions were well founded. Sally might suffer in the near future, but long term she would be better off without a man like Mike Chancery. If he could not make Sally happy before marriage what hope was there for her after the novelty of the wedding had worn off? He wasn't Sally's type and never had been. It was the attraction of complete opposites, but without the advantage that they complemented one another. Mike Chancery could complement nobody, for he had nothing at all worthwhile to give.

15

Johann stepped off the boat train at Victoria and looked at the girl waving to him with a sense of shock. For months he had kept in his mind the picture of a sun-tanned, wind-swept laughing Sally, carefree, happy, young. Now it was as if he were seeing the same ghost of a girl he'd noticed on the bus the day they had first met. Her beautiful hair and most of her face were concealed by a turquoise chiffon turban. Her green eyes looked enormous and deeply set in violet shadows in a pale face.

'Sally!' he said gently, bending to kiss her hand in a gesture she had nearly forgotten. A smile parted her lips. She said with genuine warmth:

'It *is* nice to see you again, Johann. How brown you look! How well!'

It was on the tip of his tongue to say

that he wished he could return the compliment, but something prevented him. He felt instinctively that Sally was unhappy and because he still loved her, he was at once sensitive to her desire for reticence. She would talk to him when she felt like it. Until then, he would ask no questions.

Together they changed platforms and caught a train down to Sussex. Johann talked easily about Austria. After the end of the ski-ing season he had returned to Vienna. He had been to the opera. He had seen *The Sound of Music*. Had Sally seen the film? Did she recognise the song from the film, 'Edelweiss', which had been played so frequently in Zürs.

Time passed quickly and without awkwardness. Sally, who had been anxious — nervous that Johann would seem a stranger after so long a time — began to relax. It was as if she and Johann had picked up the threads exactly where they had dropped them three months before. It was hard to believe that a friendship lasting only two weeks could have taken such deep root as to survive such a gap in time.

'It *is* nice to see you!' she said again.

Johann reached up his hand and gently touched the scarf round her head.

'It would be nice to see you!' he said, softly teasing. The colour swept into Sally's cheeks. For a moment he wondered if he had offended her, but suddenly she smiled and pulled the scarf from her head, shaking free the fair golden hair.

'There!' she said. 'That better?'

'Much!' They smiled at one another. 'No one I have met have the such pretty hair as you.' Johann added gravely. 'It is a large pity not to show it.'

Sally sighed. She had forgotten how complimentary Johann could be. It was wonderfully restorative. Lately she had been feeling anything but attractive.

She looked at the man sitting opposite her and found herself smiling again. He didn't look at all English. His suit was of continental cut and he was wearing a checked shirt and Tyrolean-type hat which he balanced on his long thin knees. He looked as if he belonged to the out-of-doors. It was only now she realised she had never seen him in anything but ski clothes. They suited him magnificently but he looked nice, if strange, in ordinary clothes.

'I have thinked I will buy English clothes when I am here in your country,' he told her. 'In Vienna most of the young men are wearing jeans and nearly all the girls wear mini-skirts. It is nice for girls with beautiful legs like yours, Sally. I think all the English mens on the train is very jealous because I accompany such attractive young lady. Perhaps they do not like that foreign man have the companies of their girls?'

'I don't suppose they mind. English-men are different — I don't think they notice me the way you do, Johann!'

There was the faintest trace of bitterness in her tone but Johann chose to ignore it.

'I will have so much the pleasure to meet your aunt,' he said. 'It is most good that she have me in her house when I am a stranger.'

'She's going to love you!' Sally said warmly.

And, of course, Aunt Margaret did. Within two days she had become Johann's slave. His charm, his beautiful manners, his thoughtfulness were all certain winners. Nor did it escape the astute middle-aged woman how Sally became a different person in his company. She laughed far more often; she was relaxed and perfectly at ease. The two young people went for long walks together; hired ponies and went riding together across the South Downs; took picnics to the seaside. Sally began to lose her pallor and to regain the tan she had abroad.

Mike's name was never mentioned. He did not ring up, and as far as Margaret Marsden knew, he had not written. Such behaviour from a fiancé was so extraordinary that she felt she must speak of it to Sally. When she had her alone on Johann's third evening, she brought up the subject casually.

'Oh we agreed not to try to keep in touch while Johann is here. I knew I'd be out a lot and Mike's terribly busy,' Sally said in an off-hand manner. But her green eyes were no longer laughing.

'Aren't you going to arrange for him and Johann to meet?' her aunt asked. 'Surely Johann will think it very rude if you don't?'

'Maybe!' Sally said vaguely and, excusing herself, went out of the room.

Alone in her own bedroom, Sally sat down on the edge of the bed and tried to calm the hurried beating of her heart. It was absurd to become so upset by her aunt's few casual references to Mike. It was time she managed to get her emotions under better control.

But she didn't want to be made to think about Mike. It was too painful ... too disturbing. Perhaps soon she would have to find the courage to face the truth about Mike and herself, but not yet. She was reasonably sure he was not having an affair with the girl Candy! The thought was so abhorrent she tried to forget it. Since their afternoon in the park together, Mike had neither telephoned nor tried to see her. All efforts to meet had come from her and Mike had been almost cruelly evasive. Pride and a reluctance to face the truth had prevented her from tackling him openly about Candy. She wasn't going to lose what last remnants of pride he'd left her by begging him to see her. Sooner or later he'd have to explain. If he'd fallen out of love with her, he'd tell her soon enough without her forcing the issue.

Suddenly Sally's face filled with angry colour. For the first time she understood the reason why Mike was deliberately trying to avoid a meeting. He was waiting for *her* to release him from an engagement he no longer wanted. He hadn't been able to find the courage to let her down a second time so now he was waiting for her to set him free.

She drew a deep breath and clasped her hands tightly in her lap. Now that she had finally admitted the thought it was all too easy to accept the fact — Mike no longer loved her. He hadn't really been in love with her for a long time. He'd just desired her. When she'd refused to meet his physical demands, he'd slowly lost interest. All the loving things he had said had only been a means to an end. She'd been taken in, tricked by her own desperate longing to believe that he really loved her as she loved him.

'He didn't blind me, I blinded myself!' Sally thought, lost in her own private agony. 'He never did love me — right from the start. I knew it after the accident and still I wouldn't see it. I've been a fool, a blind, stupid fool!'

Tears of mortification filled her eyes and spilled down her cheeks. This was the end of years of loving on her part — a bitter foreseeable end if she had only faced the truth when first it showed itself. Because she had loved

Mike so terribly, she had not been able to face up to a life in which he did not return that love as fully as she gave hers.

But *did* she really love him? Could she love a man who was so shallow, so unreliable and, at times, so cruel? He had been cruel. She had blinded herself to that, too, telling herself that his constant references to her scarred face were justified; that because if affected his work it naturally affected him, too. But now she saw that no one really in love could have behaved as Mike had done. The very last thing a lover would want to do was to criticise or hurt the person they loved. Mike had made her feel useless, unattractive, unwanted at a time when he should have been trying to do the very opposite.

She brushed the tears from her eyes and closing them, tried to picture Mike's face. It came to her; blurred, misty, pale, the blue eyes sullen, sulky, the sensuous mouth angry, demanding. What was it about this face that attracted her — had attracted her? What was there about the man himself that had made her want to spend the rest of her life at his side? What did they have in common? So little, really! Aunt Margaret had said so and she hadn't wanted to see it. Now she did. She'd been happier these three days with Johann than she'd been in two years with Mike. The simplest, most un-sophisticated things pleased and amused them. They had had moments of real intellectual companionship, too, listening to a concert in Brighton; watching ballet one evening on TV. Tomorrow they were going sailing. Johann had learned to sail as a boy on the Austrian lakes and had made arrangements to take her down to the south coast and hire a boat.

'It is necessary I find way to spend this money you repay me for the drums,' he had told her, laughing. 'So we make best fun we can with it, no?'

Fun! It was a word Johann used often and one which had not often been part of Sally's vocabulary recently. She had almost forgotten what it was to laugh. She could hear Johann singing downstairs — his voice rich and deep and boyishly unselfconscious. He seemed perfectly at home here with her and Aunt Margaret. He'd just returned from a walk into the village.

'I have record I wish to buy,' he'd told her. 'I do not know if village shop will provide, but I try.'

He wouldn't tell her what it was — it was to be a surprise. He was full of little surprises — for Aunt Margaret, too. He'd brought her a tiny Edelweiss plant in his suitcase because Sally had once told him Aunt Margaret liked gardening.

The cottage was small and the rooms far from sound-proof. Sally could hear Johann in the sitting-room beneath her bedroom. The singing had stopped now and she could hear music — the record Johann had bought in the village and was playing on the old record player.

It was a Viennese waltz — one which

she had heard often in Zürs and to which she and Johann had danced.

'Sally? Sally?' His voice calling her carried up to her room. 'Come down here and dance with me, Sally. If you do not come at once, I shall dance with your aunt!'

His voice was full of laughter, full of an easy happiness. Despite the tears still wet on her cheeks, Sally smiled. 'I'll be down in a minute!' she called back.

She went over to the dressing-table to wipe away the traces of her tears. Down below she could hear Aunt Margaret protesting that she was far too old to dance. Johann was brooking no refusal.

'Is easy, no? Everything is easy when you try a little,' he said. 'You do the waltz nearly so good as Sally. She is very beautiful dancer and very beautiful girl, too.'

Sally's cheeks flushed. Did Johann realise she could hear him? Perhaps he had meant her to hear.

She reached up and lifted the curtain of fair hair away from her face. The scar showed faintly on her cheek. She thought of Johann's long gentle fingers as they had once touched her face in Zürs, and suddenly she realised that this man was of a very different calibre from Mike. It was strange that she could become attracted by two such total opposites. They were not only opposite in appearance but in all their ways. Johann was gentle, quiet, thoughtful, seemingly placid; Mike quick, dynamic, moody and temperamental. Where Johann was physically energetic, Mike was artistically so. Where Mike was demanding, Johann was giving.

Sally sighed. She recalled a quotation from Shakespeare's *Much Ado About Nothing* — Comparisons are odious. Perhaps it was wrong to compare the two men, yet having the warmth of Johann's friendship, admiration and affection helped her to see Mike in a new light. A true light? Sally wondered. Was Mike really shallow, egotistical and selfish? And was her heart quite so completely broken as she supposed by the realisation that Mike did not love her? Was loving him just a habit? Nothing more?

She went downstairs in a strangely thoughtful mood. Sensitive as always to her feelings, Johann took care of the conversation so that there was no effort in being in his company. Gradually, as they talked and occasionally danced, she felt her mood lighten. The problem of what to do about Mike receded to the back of her mind — an unpleasant, unhappy decision that could be dealt with tomorrow or the next day. Now, with Aunt Margaret smiling and happy and Johann telling her how beautifully she danced, she would not waste the hours with any more self-analysis or regrets. Despite everything, she was happy for this moment in time. Only a fool would waste happiness when it was there within one's grasp.

But the evening was not fated to remain so calm and serene in its contentment. The telephone bell rang shrilly in the hall at nine o'clock. Aunt

Margaret answered it and came back into the room to inform Sally that Mike wished to speak to her.

For a moment Sally stood hesitatingly in the encirclement of Johann's arms, their dancing arrested. Her face filled slowly with colour. She was not aware of it, but her fingers had tightened imperceptibly on Johann's arm as if she were clinging to him for support. Aunt Margaret said:

'Would you like me to tell him you are out?'

Sally let out her breath.

'No!' she said. 'Of course not . . . '

She released herself from Johann's arms and went out of the room, closing the door behind her. When she picked up the receiver, her hand was trembling.

'Sally?' Mike's voice sounded impatient. 'I've been trying to get you for the last hour. Where have you been?'

'Here!' Sally answered, her throat suddenly dry. 'We've had the record player on. Perhaps that's why we didn't hear the phone ringing.'

'Sounds as if you're having an amusing time down there!' Now Mike sounded jealous. 'Darling, if it's all right with you, I thought I'd come down tomorrow and see you. It's been such ages, my sweet. I can't wait another day.'

Sally's eyebrows lifted in surprise. His suggestion was so unexpected it was a moment or two before she could believe he meant it.

'Mike, I can't . . . I mean, it isn't a good day . . . I mean . . . well, I'm going sailing tomorrow with Johann. We'll be out all day.'

Now there was silence from Mike's end of the wire — as if he, in his turn, could not believe Sally's words. When he spoke, his voice was sharp, petulant.

'Surely you can go sailing another day? I'm busy on Wednesday and tomorrow's my only free day. Besides, I *want* to see you, Sally.'

She ought to have felt thrilled. But the first tiny moment of triumph was replaced at once by a feeling of resentment. Mike had made no effort to get in touch with her for days. Now, because he had nothing better to do he expected her to cancel all her plans just for the pleasure of spending a few hours with him.

'I'm sorry, Mike, but I can't alter anything. It wouldn't be fair to Johann.'

'Oh damn Johann!' Mike exploded. 'Whose fiancée are you anyway? His or mine?'

'You haven't objected to my entertaining Johann before now,' Sally rejoined sharply. 'Why this sudden change?'

There was another brief silence. Sally realised Mike might have been shocked at her tone of voice. He wasn't used to it from her. She expected an angry retort but, surprisingly, Mike's voice was gentle, coaxing.

'Darling, don't be like that. I know I've been rather neglectful lately, but I've been up to my eyes. Honestly, my sweet, I just haven't had a moment. But that doesn't mean I haven't been thinking about you. I have — all the time. I never wanted you to have that fellow staying with you. You must know that. I just didn't think it fair to you to object when you were so keen to have him. I thought you'd think I was being selfish or old-fashioned or something.'

'I wouldn't have thought any of those things,' Sally said, as much to herself as to him. 'I'd have thought you were reacting like any fiancé — like any man in love.'

'Darling, don't let's *quarrel!*' Mike said, 'It isn't a bit fair to me. Here I am ringing you up to tell you how much I love you and you're behaving as if you don't even like me any more.'

'I'm not sure that I do!'

The words were out before she could consider them. Now that they were spoken, she found she had no wish to retract them. She wasn't sure she did like him.

'Sally, what *is* wrong with you? You've changed. What's happened? Is this your way of punishing me because I haven't had time to see much of you lately? If so, I think it's pretty rotten of you. When people love each other, they are supposed to try to understand each other. *You* know how busy I get. It isn't my fault.'

'Too busy to make one phone call? Write one letter?' Sally asked bitterly. 'You talk of love, Mike, and people understanding each other. When did you last stop to think how I have been feeling lately?'

'Darling you *are* cross with me!' Mike sounded almost relieved. 'And quite right, too. I've been a selfish brute. I'm coming down tomorrow to see you. I'll show you just how sorry I am, my sweet. We'll have a perfect day together, just the two of us . . . '

'Mike, I'm going sailing with Johann. I can't see you.'

'Don't be stubborn, Sally. Of course you can if you want to. Tell him you'll go another day. Tell him I'm insisting, as your fiancé, on having first claim on your time.'

'No, Mike! I won't disappoint Johann. I don't even want to do so, I'm looking forward to tomorrow.'

This time the silence lasted over a minute. When Mike next spoke Sally could detect the anger underlying the measured tone of his voice.

'You're beginning to make me feel you don't love me any more. What's been going on between you and that Austrian? Answer me, Sally!'

'I don't think I owe you any explanations, Mike.' Sally replied quietly, 'I've never asked you to make any, though many times I think I would have been justified in doing so.'

'He's been setting you against me — or that aunt of yours has!' Mike said furiously, ignoring her remark.

'No one has said a word against you, Mike. If you really want to know, you are the only person who has ever influenced me as to how I feel about you. But not this time. This time I've found out for myself that you aren't worth loving. I'm breaking our engagement,

Mike. I no longer want to be married to you.'

She had not known she was going to make that speech. The words came as if they were from someone else; from some other Sally buried down below the girl she thought she was, someone who had been slowly drowning but was now coming up towards the surface; towards light, life itself.

'You can't mean that. I need you, Sally. You can't walk out on me now. I love you. I've always loved you. There's never been anyone else but you. Sally, listen to me . . . '

'I'm sorry, Mike. I've nothing more to say. It's all finished. I never want to see you again — never.'

Now that she had begun to throw off the shackles that had weighed her down for so long, she was finding it breathtakingly easy. She no longer felt angry, hurt, surprised, doubtful. She knew with a positive irrevocable certainty that this is what she should have done years ago. Her love for Mike had been a tortuous unhappy desperate kind of loving, without joy, without real faith, without even real friendship as its basis. She had nothing now to give him; nothing she wanted from him except to be allowed to forget him.

Mike seemed unable, or unwilling, to credit her words.

'You don't mean it. You can't mean it!' he said over and over again. When finally he realised that she was in earnest, he suddenly became abrasive.

'This is your way of getting back at me. You found out about Candy. Admit it, Sally. You're jealous. You want to make me unhappy because you're jealous of Candy. Well, it's finished. I give you my word on that, Sally. I'd never meant to have an affair with her — it was only because she . . . '

'I don't want to hear about her!' Sally broke in violently, 'I'm not interested in the sordid details of your life, Mike. Find yourself another girl. Maybe someone else will think you are worth loving, I don't!'

He began to offer excuses but sickened to the pit of her stomach, Sally could not bear to listen. Quietly she replaced the receiver, cutting off the sound of his voice. She stood in the hall, shivering. She hadn't known about Candy. Perhaps deep down she had suspected something of the kind, but she had not wanted to face the thought. Now that Mike had confessed of his own accord, she could feel nothing but a deep sense of relief that she had told him she was breaking their engagement even before she'd known the full extent of his worthlessness. Somehow it salved her pride that she had reached her decision before she heard the humiliating fact that even as her fiancé, he'd had so little respect for her that he could indulge in a sordid affair with another girl. She neither knew nor cared whether Candy or Mike had broken off the association. It didn't matter. It didn't matter because she just didn't care.

'I don't care!' Sally whispered. Her

sense of release was so intense she wanted to shout the words aloud. Instead, she went back into the sitting-room and met Aunt Margaret's anxious eyes with a smile.

'Sorry to be so long,' she said in a calm voice which utterly belied the tumult of her inner feelings. 'But I've just broken off my engagement to Mike and it took a bit of time getting him to understand that I meant it.'

Her aunt jumped to her feet like a young girl, her face radiant. She hugged Sally joyfully.

'Oh, darling, I'm so glad!' she whispered.

'So am I!' said Sally.

Over Aunt Margaret's head, she could see Johann staring at her intently, a smile crinkling the corners of his mouth and eyes.

'It is finished, your betrothal, for always?' he asked.

'For always!' Sally answered firmly.

'That is good!' said Johann. He began searching in the pocket of his jacket for the little dictionary he always carried with him.

'There is the English word I do not know and wish to say,' he said, leafing through the pages. Presently he found the word he wanted. He turned to Aunt Margaret and gave her a formal little bow.

'Now that Sally is free, I request your permission, dear lady, to woo your niece?' He gave her an anxious glance. 'This is the right word, no?'

'Yes, definitely *yes!*' said Aunt Margaret, laughing in spite of herself. 'You have my permission, Johann, and my blessing, too.'

Johann turned to Sally.

'And you, Sally?' he asked. 'You do not have the objections either? For the long time I have known myself to love you, always I have kept myself from so saying because you were affianced to another man. Now I wish you greatly to know how I feel. I love you since the first day I see you. I love you all the time in Zürs and now when I come to

England, I am loving you still. You do not mind?'

'No!' Sally left her aunt's side and put her hand trustingly in Johann's as he held it out to her. 'I am very touched and proud that you should love me. I don't know if I can return your love. But I want to, Johann. I like you so very much and I am always happy in your company.'

Johann looked deeply into Sally's big green eyes. His face broke into a smile.

'It is but a small step from there to love,' he said. 'So already you make me the hopeful and happy man.'

Then, disregarding Aunt Margaret's presence, he kissed her. The kiss lay warm and tender on her scarred cheek.